Sonata for Piano and Violin

A novel by Matthew Gasda

Serpent Club Press

Serpent Club Press books may be purchased for educational, business, or sales promotional use. For more information please contact Serpent Club Press at theserpentclub@gmail.com

First Edition

Printed in the United States of America
Set in Williams Caslon
Designed by Emily Gasda

ISBN-13
978-0-9906643-2-1

ISBN-10
0990664325

LCCN
2015901887

Other works from Serpent Club Press:

2013

Moon on Water
Matthew Gasda

2014

Autumn, Again; Spring, Anew
Michael Skelton and Stephen Morel

On Bicycling: An Introduction
Samuel Atticus Steffen

For E.G. and D.B.

Sonata for Piano and Violin

And then, unheard-of-marvel, the two artists, plunged in gloom and performed the last three movements from memory, with a fire and passion the more astounding to the listeners in that there was an absence of all externals which could enhance the performance. Music, wondrous and alone, held sovereign sway in the darkness of night.

- Vincent d'Indy (recalling a night of music in 1886)

It may perhaps be many years before some of the most sublime realizations of yourself ... will rise to the surface like remembrances and reveal the deep logic that holds man and artist, life and dream together. I for my part am now certain of what you are: and this is for me the most personal aspect of this book, that I believe us to be allies in the difficult secrets of living and dying, at one in that sense of the eternal that binds human beings together. From now on you can depend on me.

- Lou Andreas-Salomé (letter to Rainer Maria Rilke)

I. *Allegretto ben moderato*

because of this feeling I have today that life brings us back to our fate and that we are like the sky and the trees and the immense oceans of rain beyond the evenings of darkening and it was beautiful today wasn't it? seeing him and not saying anything and him looking at me with eyes of saltwater and ash to the years when the city was falling apart and we were in love: the years before we started making the choices that turned us into the kinds of people that we swore (absolutely swore) we'd never become

remembering when he came in from the rain and we made love with our mouths open and spit dripped onto the floor and I swore that I'd never been happier (and was it happiness wasn't it?) with the sunlight pouring in from literally everywhere and it was a Sunday in the spring: and that's what life comes to (a pattern that doesn't repeat itself except in memory)

only this single musical phrase seeking another voice to join itself with (if only)

his voice very quiet subtle-soft: reading the poems that remembered me as one would remember flowers and I thought about something he said to me when we were fifteen (it was about love) and did he recognize me today? he must've (and I know I've gone a little soft around the eyes and mouth but even then I and then that initial "let" authorizing the logic of pain my voice over the phone telling him that I'd left him for Richard so many years ago now (and the clouds reflected on the glass buildings are themselves a second sky)

something I copied down from one of the poems today :

Mariel looks like a blue violin
drowned in the bathtub
her strings combed out like hair

everything we experience becomes a river that we may swim in beginning only afterwards (after the dark uptake of the brutal present) and my understanding of who he was is just a reflection of this deep unmet desire to be completely transformed by him and by the love we had when I was almost a child (15) and by the poems which were accidentals along the scales of our touch

his thoughts like clouds passing under his eyes

and then outside smoking I see that he left his email address in the front of my book instead of the autograph he gave everyone else and I wonder why? maybe because his heart was in his throat seeing me walk in not looking so bad even at my age (55) and it's possible (I'm thinking it's possible)

and it's like we are carrying time like water across a desert and he sounds like a broken instrument when he reads his poems and I feel like he's singing from within trying to go past some limit imposed on us by the past and does he remember what I was like at fifteen? how I panicked at everything panicked when my mother picked us up from school panicked when my father moved out panicked when my grades dropped panicked when I got the lead in the school play panicked when I met him at The Met panicked when he started talking about French films I had never heard of and Renoir and Hart Crane (still his favorite poet I'm sure): and does he remember that I had to go to a therapist twice a week because for three years of my life (from ages eight to eleven) I never spoke to anyone including my parents? and does he remember how I hated my therapist? or how the two of us used to laugh about the crazy things I told my therapist ? knowing that Freudians needed neurotic rich girls more than neurotic rich girls needed Freudians

and at fifteen if a girl is sad there can only be hysteria (because she isn't allowed to be JUST sad) and what bullshit that was because I was just plain unhappy when I met him but he made me feel so good because he wrote poems on napkins and because he knew something about everything and because his father was a writer and because he was older and because he read dead languages and because he had nice hair and teeth and because he liked to kiss me and because I found it completely unnerving how much he wanted to kiss me (because I wasn't used to that) and when my parents got divorced I didn't care when my analyst told me that I should care that there was something wrong with my not caring just like there was with my not speaking to anyone at all but I thought that was bullshit: that people should be allowed to do things they aren't supposed to do and he (P) was the first person to tell me it was OK to do what I wanted (and that was to his advantage too of course (to encourage me))

and why I am remembering all this now? everything that he wrote and I did: everything that was heroically lost and heroically found:

my body forced to move to the tempo of his voice

a verb trying to find a tense yes like a tempo it's more like 9/8 than the old 4/4 today trying to transcribe this feeling of having fractured myself along the lines of

those evenings of beautiful glooms our tongues overlapping speaking into the heart beating like mad

reading online this morning about his reading (the reading to be given at the bookstore in SOHO)

meaning I had to lie to Richard: saying 'I have this work thing' that I'll be home late and 'not to worry'

the twistedness of a lie like a sapling torn up by the roots:

root systems never being as dedicated to the ground as they are to the sky his famous hands undoing my hair: pushing me onto the bed

and once (as I recall) he spit in my mouth and slapped me across the face and I had to turn face down on the bed (to conceal my happiness)

fucking for the first time I bled all over and both of us thought it was so funny and so heavy at the same time (all that blood like a sign of our mortality) and he was so kind (wiping my thighs down washing the sheets making up a lie for his father (who didn't need to be lied to anyway because his father was so kind and understanding))

magnificently palpable but not so visible: the natural desire of the heart

and even now I don't want to admit to having seen him today and to this chain of remembrances being set off like a series of fireworks lined up in a row

because we had music in the evenings on the record player and there was impressionistic sunlight pouring in from all the windows (and the windows on the doors) and I hope that I have copies of his books somewhere at home especially the first one (the one that's so much about about me and our love) (that crazy love)): his slim little light blue books all of which have the same binding

and I always imagined them like petals abandoned not on the metro but in space and time

*and no I don't want that desperate music now because of
how much pain there is and was (the imminence of death
and all that) and because of how little chance we have
of healing and of starting over (of recycling ourselves of
renewing our faith in*

*so I imagine that loving him would be like making collages
out of cut paper (white flowers like drops of milk) and he
used to say that he'd compose poems for me out of birdsong
and air and I remember him saying once that he wished
that I'd break his heart so that he could write to me about
it later*

*as if it were possible to trace the movement of time like the
path of a bird across the white of a cloud*

*(because fearless fearless fearless the soul that will wound
itself to death)*

*going to his house in Brooklyn Heights listening to his father
talk about Schubert (or about German writers or English
poets or French films) and that first spring was so lovely
and he used to sit in a big plush green old chair and watch
me talk to his father and I always wondered what he was
thinking (if he was composing a poem in his head) and
we listened to Joni Mitchell records (we both loved Joni)
and in the dark we liked to make love to Debussy and his
record collection had some of those wonderful preludes and
arabesques and it was all grace and light: because that's
what I remember as much as the sex the music the*

on a piece of paper I once wrote down a question that I submitted to my mother ('why does a girl who does not speak need speech therapy?') and to my family I was the silent girl as much as I was the fearless girl (which is what P called me) and in his poems about silence (alpine flowers blooming on a spring day et cetera) he refers to me over and over in variously oblique ways

and when I got the role of Puck in the school play (my school refusing to let boys from other schools play any of the parts) he came and watched me and I don't think he ever heard me talk as much as I did that night when I said those magical things onstage and after that night I think I began to talk more: maybe because of him and maybe because of Shakespeare and maybe just because I wanted to

and I never saw a man as emotional as him (he carried himself with a certain SOMETHING and I liked it (that that certain something) and whatever it was was something from within: his ridiculous insistence on having beauty in his life (and order)

and until I turn blue I'll remember the way we'd fall asleep (on his roof) under the stars (invisible in New York) not moving until the dawn woke us up and unconcealed our bodies covered in sweat: our fingers locked and folded together like reeds in a stream *because each person only gets a few themes: a few strains (a few chords) to play for the rest of their lives and for me I guess it's*

only it was not long before I met him that I obtained breasts and hips (that almost-exquisite beauty that embarrassed me and that I never knew what to do with) and it was only just after I met him that I started cutting pictures from Vogue magazine and pasting them over my bedroom walls and I know he looked down on it (my reading magazines like Vogue) but I'm sure he read about baseball or something completely boyish and American and everyone has secret quotidian life of their own (and I don't think that he ever accepted that about people and that's why he became a poet I think: to hide his soul away from the crushing smallness of everyone around him)

an inner-ripple of light spreading across the mind because suddenly I'm willing to let myself go back to THAT time

and in those days my father was living in a rundown apart near Gramercy Park with Melissa who was practically my age: Melissa who was an actress in one of his plays: Melissa who used to give me wine and whiskey and cigarettes: Melissa who played beebop records all night: Melissa who I imagined my father loved because he was the kind of helpless older man who falls for mysterious (and vain) actresses who need sentimental old men and I liked her because she wasn't as serious as

*other people I knew then and because she didn't treat me
like someone who had a million problems and because she
made fun of therapists too and*

*maybe she was a product of the times but it was nice
having someone like an older sister (because my own
older sister Clara was awful to me because she was
always so jealous and I heard she died before she was
forty it might've been heroin or love or a car accident
and who knows? (I never found out because I didn't
want to know and why would I?)*

*his letters were full of secrets especially the letters from
the first spring we were together when my mother would
spend entire evenings talking about my father's secrets all
the ways in which he was a bad and stupid and deceitful
man and I'm not sure if I ever believed anything my
mother said*

*but no I don't want to think about her: I want to think
about HIM (P) and his letters and the sideways almost
laconic things he would write to me about the fate of the
universe and I bet he hasn't changed at all (because the
only thing that changes about people are their disguises)*

*then there was my sister's boyfriend Jim who wore ties
and talked about famous existentialists (Jim was a real
drag and I used to think it was so funny when P did
his impression of Jim) and it was because I was an
extraordinarily bright young women (in the words of my*

favorite teacher Mr. Matthews) that I once (politely) told Jim to go and fuck himself

because I've always been like that (thinking about it now): the kind of person who sees through bullshit but cannot stop it

and what is that pattern that springs from tranquil almost quiet evenings alone? an enthusiasm for sex or transcendence? accretions of clouds? affections? wrinkles rainy days? concern with the preservation of our beautiful half-over lives? the integration of consciousness with desire? (or is it something ELSE (something even more mysterious) that has brought me back to him again and again like a nocturnal creature lost abroad in the evening)

a love like renewal and nothing like it at the same time (a love like bleeding without losing any blood)

and he called me the fearless girl because of the way I made love to him

splitting me open sucking the juices out with his lips and tongue while I'm talking to him telling him how to consume me and no one is as unserious as I am: jumping through hoops just to feel alive (frivolous-girl madwomen dancer) he never knew this but I wrote him hundreds of letters which I left carefully bundled in the second floor ladies room of The Met hoping that someone would find them who was romantic enough to read them and I liked the idea of having my own personal mystery-aura: of having some kind of Byronic allure around me like I was someone else: someone I actually wanted to be: and is there anyone out there who has never really wanted to be someone other than themselves?

because I'm falling away perpetually from the single point that I've been trying to arrive at: that single point that I am failing to articulate as we speak:

how his body tasted (sour) or how it smelled (like roses and rain) and how he whistled at death and how he meditated on the clouds between the trees and how sensitive (how natural) he was (and how perceptive) and how his roses were auditory (singing laughing crying) and how his eyes were full of blueish light

those first poems are written to me on napkins but later he progressed to fastfood menus scraps of newspaper magazines and eventually he made it all the way to clean sheets of paper and one day he demanded that I burn everything he ever gave me (and I did of course I did: I did anything he asked of me) because my devotion was unique to the universe I believed (and still believe): unique because it was real (unique because it was actually devotion)

honeysuckle lobes broken by thunder my toes curling at the sound of the rain and that feeling (returning to me again after so so many years now) of physical completeness (the shell of hollow pearl he called Agape)

and again and again I return to this music: but the kernel of the sacred will not open

because I never loved my mother that was the problem (not for a second) and she knew it and she never believed that anyone ever loved her and that was her problem (the old self-fulfilling prophecy the pattern in people that manifests itself like

that gentleness (that receptivity) to everything that's what I'd like to have now and look how it slips through our fingers like rain (so sorrowfully) and so gently (life) so distracted by the scent the

bloom of youth blown over the river I remember the fragrance grubbed up by pollution on the surface of the water (our undistilled love our Dandelion wine)

my mother's boyfriend buying me Vogues to make me happy the Vogues I liked to cut pictures out of: his name was Eliot and I really think he loved my mother even if she never knew it and he never saw her flaws and he stayed by her side up until the day she died and if he did see her flaws he was kind enough to look away

because Eliot was a nice man who had a big apartment on Central Park West which was good for me because we got out of the shithole (which was all my poor mother could afford after the divorce) and because I had the crucial bit of extra space then to just relax and stare at a wall or read or just let the silence sink through me like sunlight and a human life accrues kindnesses like debt and there's never anyone or anyway to pay the debt back is there?

('my poor mother': isn't that what every daughter thinks about her mother after her mother's died?

and it was unfortunate that the brief period in which I was incredibly beautiful coincided with the year he met me and it would've been so much easier if he had not wanted to possess me (to fuck me) so badly

or maybe that's just what I told myself or allowed myself to believe while I gave into it (the poetry of hunger)

'today wasn't easy as I didn't get a letter from you' I remember writing to him once (and it wasn't ('today'))

the mystery of a city like New York is that it is terrible and doesn't it love us the way we love it

spreading the fabric of time smooth with his hand calling me his springtime girl and what an idiot I was for letting my whole life go by like the way it has and how lovely it was when he kissed me on the mouth and on my neck and told me that he loved me and how simple the way he came between my fingers or in my mouth or inside the part of me that he said was like an orchid opening to the evening

and now I am silence-haunted because the language we spoke is dead: implicated in our own (and very real) desire

and I've lived my whole life for rainwater and salt and the music which curls off the wind

flushing the evenings with stars

and he (P) was the first person to take me seriously (outside of my teacher Mr. Matthews) and that meant everything to me (not being treated like a child: being treated like someone serious with serious ideas serious feelings serious ideas about How To Live) and for the rest of my life I've) been waiting to be recognized again like I was by him

but I never compared him (P) to Mr. Matthews because not matter what anybody ever said: they were in completely different categories for me and still are

P never made jokes and yet he came across as incredibly winning: which is to say that people liked him despite who he was and with sex games being natural to us we fucked every possible way we could think of: and I pushed back against him with all my strength not wanting to lose myself completely in him

there were limits when there could be no limits with a love like we had

and I was bitterly jealous because my friends were so beautiful and cultured and I was nothing like that (because I was nothing in general) just a sad girl with a secret boyfriend who wished all the time that she was someone else (anyone else)

but underneath he was so selfish (even in the beginning)

after I got of school we went to the movies almost everyday or we'd go to Central Park and lay around and talk about the books he was reading or the books I was reading and I still have a book by my nightstand all the time and I take them with me on the train because he taught me how to really read (with my whole soul) and even when I was performing every night in the theater I would read in my dressing room because I guess I was trying to understand him or understand myself or just UNDERSTAND for the sake of understanding but now I realize (with my life half over) that I haven't understood a thing about literature or him or myself or

failing to gain any wisdom: unaccrued like a bank account stuck at zero (despite a lifetime of faithful deposits)

19

the film version his novel The Dancer which I must have gone to see a million times with a young Daniel Day-Lewis playing the P-role and it was almost cruel seeing us portrayed like that (seeing myself like that from distance)

because I was played with more frailty than I really displayed in real life:

because I was tougher than THAT: at least on the outside (at least to other people)

but even now there's often this movement to stay in bed and hide under the covers like a small child

dragging a flock of animals to sacrifice (how I imagine the director treating the actors in that film)

the first spring was the only spring for me: there were always lasts but he was the first

because he said I tasted like the rain and because he noticed the light in me and because I noticed the light in him and because he understood me the second he saw me (wandering around half-lost in the Metropolitan Museum of Art asking strangers where I could find the Van Goghs)

and the emotion of today is like the beginning of a universe

the iris then the honeysuckle opening (I remember it all)

parted from me leaf by leaf reconstructed in the air

wound like birdsong into the dark

then when I had a child I forced myself to stop thinking about these things (about my own youth in general I guess)

and Julian is older than P was when I met him and it's almost amazing to think that there are these patterns within us that replicate themselves and pass themselves on into the future

and I can only imagine that someone looking at my life objectively would find my relationship with my son deeply imperfect or imperfectly formed: because I was always (in a way) trying to replace the love that I had given up with P

and however psychologically perverse that might seem (no matter how unfair to Julian) subjectively speaking (because life is lived in the subjective tense and everyone knows it) I had no other choice

because we're left standing amidst the withered shells of what we were trying to keep ourselves from (disintegration and despair)

passing through a memory like a car through a mountain tunnel:

not able to adjust to the loss of natural light fast enough:
not happy at having lost the radio signal momentarily

the sharp lines in his cheeks obvious underneath the
stubble today the graying of his hair enobling but sad too
(more sad than enobling really)

just like I was afraid of: just like I secretly projected
when I used to imagine how the image of our lives would
evolve

touch being the only real way we spoke to one another

like we'd created a game called it 'presence' (or symmetry)
dug our hands under our ribs ripped the sculpture of the
heart to pieces and I'd always bloom (unreasonably) in
the evening with the sun dying away and he'd put his
fingers in my mouth let me bite down enough to hurt but
not enough to draw blood and sometimes I drew blood
anyway because he secretely wanted me to

and then my mother would call hysterically angry asking
why I wasn't home yet and I don't think she really cared
about where I was or whether I was safe et cetera but
was just taking the opportunity (the opportunity of my
being off somewhere completely in love) to exert her
power over me

and it scared me I think to realize that my intuitions
about him were essentially correct (that he was the

genius he claimed he was) and how frightening it was to live like that: like we were on fire

then a decade ago reading about his father's death I

AND when I read he was doing a reading at such-and-such bookstore how could I not think about going?

AND how could I not decide to do more than just think?

because in the end thinking doesn't count for anything and even if actions don't either at least I could say to myself that I tried: which in the moment of the temporal absolute (the moment of NOW) is worth something

each thought circling back into the previous thought I guess like a diminishing or expanding loop I can never tell which

and I want to at least be able to stop wondering if he reads notices of my plays or about the awards I've won or the films I appeared in or of the life I've lead (so happy so content) with Richard (who became a big success even if everything he ever directed was boring as hell)

or did he (P) ignore my career completely (forgoing his claim to having fucked (and fucked very well) a famous stage actress in her prime)?

like a wound in the earth like sunlight like rainwater o'

because I am disgraced by the silence that I feel

faith chasing after a shape like a tree chasing after a seed:

or like the note I wrote to him that I intended to slip into his hand at the signing and which I failed to do:

'Whether or not I can hold you or not it carries me almost inexplicably back light or dust or anything borne from shadow I would still fashion for you all the parachutes my small hands could bear because you may be enamoured by silhouettes (with their burdens) but the silhouettes inside themselves run down to the centre exhaustingly (and you may become so exquisitely overwhelmed) and I lose you in them (because I lost you in them once) but here I am P here I am'

and so bless me my body erotic strife these lamentations not of the woman but of the fissured self when I was sixteen asking him to sodomize me on his writing desk one night I don't think he knew what to believe but he did it anyway because we did those kinds of things (because we had this erotic mania that bore itself out in acts that we didn't believe we were capable of) and it was a joy it was an incredible joy the kind of joy I would trade everything for to have again

having successfully defined myself as unlimited (with him) I had no choice but to redefine myself as the most limited woman alive

because what's a body but the sum of the experiences that it contains?

o' and how we kissed: each of us brooding within the other like a kettle left hissing on the flame

because I was a fucked up girl: a hysterical girl starving for attention and yes that's the pat answer and yes life is full of pat answers and yes I'd like to resist them and yes I WILL resist them and yes I won't

but the pat (the banal) pushes its way (anyway) to the front of the line in a hurry to get home and watch TV

because he would just hang around at the Met (which was free then) and he had all kinds of different jobs and I just thought he was (if nothing else) incredibly charismatic smoking cigarettes and spouting philosophy and feigning a romantic disinterest in everyone and he was disinterested I think (because I'm old enough to give him credit for certain things now that I wasn't before)

(so the notion that I would want to spend more time with him was already there from the beginning)

and how monstrous it was of my mother never to acknowledge that she affected every single one of my moods and feelings about myself (and about him (about P))

altering my perception of men from the very start which really helped determined everything that happened when I was an adult like that famous letter to P where I revealed that I was engaged to Richard and I was in "The Seagull" then and what did he write back? nothing: he just mailed me the page from the play where Treplev shoots himself and how unsubtle I thought that was how unsubtle for an otherwise subtle artful man but it wasn't an artful thing I did leaving him for Richard and doing it secretly too (with Richard who was directing me in the play)

and yes a part of me liked the cruelty of leaving things off like that (with such finality) I needed that little rush of power then and I don't know why but I just needed it I did and in a way I don't regret it (that rush of power despite the consequences)

and I have these ideal memories of him learning German and reading Rilke to me in bed and telling me about Nietzsche and Heine and all those Germans who were so important to him: the German writers that he said were playing ball on a different level than anyone writing in English at the time

and I'm not sure that I cared then as much as he did about Beauty

delta waves after sleep just the beginning of all this:

emotions curdled like milk left out on the table

because the soul removes itself from itself like the soil removes itself from the seed and in the the activity of self-exploration (contemplating the sea of internal images discerning connections ungrammatical remarks) we

?

like a falling off into depth and then (as before) a silence a beginning (no) a nothing a nonexistence and that's what I think death is: something one slits open with one's teeth in order to watch it sprawl to the ground unborn

remembering the Sicilian almonds we unshelled and ate the lime trees we threw stones at (all of this part of the fantasy we had then of living near the sea)

because sorrow is a parasite that I have not yet reconciled to this unclosed past

because it's a confirmation of something (and something IS happening): but I neither believe in it nor care to believe in it:

the instantiation of the foregone the forelorn the

barren old age and regrets but I won't go in for that (the singing of despair) there must be something else at least there must be something to add to the despair to lessen its burden

my big slim hips thrown around him his hands pushing me onto the bed like rain thrust through a cloud his teeth revealing the taste of my lips my neck my fingers wanting to sing or shut up or just let it YES this inhuman emotion catch up to me

hanging in the trees like a bat my eyes open and the wind shaking the first flowers from the trees and both of us falling wildly to the grass then

like a message afloat on a river of smoke

I run my hands over every object in the apartment toast bottles cigarettes tablecloths and I don't feel anything except this miraculous texture of pain

(this exercise in self-forgiveness having left the man I loved: having

and I see that even poets or classicists (or whatever he is) react to competition and uncertainty the way everyone else does

because everyone farts and shits and cries and begins to smell if they don't shower for a few days

and reads their spouse's diaries and emails (just like I read Richard's)

and I've always wanted to return to my memories as a different person (because my dreams always imagine me as a better version of myself and I never told him about this never told anyone anything ever) because Richard says I make people uncomfortable and thinks that it's largely due to my unclear intentions

and it's difficult to think of writing as anything other than a representation of a non-presence

without some faith that language has a natural state that separates it from thinking (secreting) (bleeding)

so drinking is a kind of a freedom for me even if I hide it from my family and my collegues in the theater and everyone

but then again there are these alternative non-erotic visions of life like packing lunch for Julian kissing Richard on the forehead after rehearsal

the three of us not having much money in the early days and nothing else really mattered except THAT (our being together) and how quickly though it all gives way (that communal wholeness) to erotic needs and how quickly I'm back to where I was thinking about P at the bookstore reading his poems signing books looking over my shoulder like there was something just incredibly fascinating just where I wasn't (standing right in front of him)

so nearly beautiful once and so nearly alive: drawn down over the damp skin of the earth

(because where trees have roots I have legs)

and I'll carry renewal like a stone across a desert and I'll take up our love like I always knew it was there (because what does it matter if I gave my love to Richard the theater director who reminded me of my father? even if it was P who I really (always) loved) and MY GOD how awful these thoughts become: running on like this forever

because spring is a parcel of new life: and the texture of our sex was sweet and forgiving

and that's what a regret is: our understanding of the incontrovertible fact of choice

tarnished tinfoil on the counter dirty glasses half-eaten sandwiches (the days I spent cleaning up after Julian in the spare moments between rehearsals)

after I'd started to get better roles and we were able to move into the apartment (this apartment) that I consider my home as much as any place I've ever lived

and of course Richard helped secure us too (materially as a family): but I've always hated giving him credit for things (even when he deserved it)

and was I good mother? I wonder but I'll never know because I'll never have the courage to ask

but is being GOOD really what's important about being a mother? because it seems to me that (looking back) and just showing up is what really mattered (and I showed up every single day)

and my whole life has had this physical almost perfect sorrow to it this unending uncanny feeling of being somewhere else at the same time that I'm HERE somewhere ANYWHERE at any moment:

like when falling in love or acting in a play or falling out with my mother or doting on my father or falling out with my sister (who left to join an ashram anyway)

or writing my favorite English teacher a letter admitting to him that I love him that I'd always loved him since he first called on me in class

but NOT in a sexual way: in an appreciative way (like I said) because he was the only person (including P) who took me seriously in a way that I believed in as real

the fourth (musical) dimension of the universe (timelessness) making itself apparent to me all at once and I have an image of a lily in mind with a million petals which unfold (the mental lily) petal by petal so that when I do this I do not feel panic and when I was fifteen I practiced this over and over I sat alone in my room with the lights off and practiced and sometimes while I did this (unfolded the petals) I listened to my sister's records too despite her wish that I not do so and despite the usual consequence of her screaming at me at the top of her lungs

and no: no longer recognizable as someone in love

because there's this permanent openness and receptivity to change: as if from a certain point of view in space we were like bacteria wriggling and mutating and conforming to

?

my mother playing Chopin waltzes on the piano my father smoking cigarettes at Caffe Dante talking to actors about Ibsen or Chekhov and how sad my father was because he couldn't really love anyone but himself

and yet in an offhand way he was so full of love too like a character from a Russian novel: always getting sloppily drunk and expressing his unfathomable care for someone whose name he'd forgotten (or worse)

the second week we knew each other P and I decided to camp out in Central Park and live like characters in the Forest of Arden and the important thing was that for a moment we believed it was possible

and he (P) (THAT NAME) used to talk about Plato Beckett Sophocles Plato Kafka Shakespeare Joyce Crane Rimbaud blah blah blah and at times he sounded like any other young New York intellectual trying to fuck a teenage girl who took extra French lessons after school

through each other we felt that wider radiance of being alive during those late spring nights on the weekends dirt and flowers in Prospect Park his father bringing us sandwiches and coffee on the roof and the jazz records and wine at night before falling asleep and I was the best I ever was then the best self I'd ever be and even after my son was born I still thought of him and how his letters were like torn up notes (scraps of eternity) and how they floated over me like bits of dust and how I'd let him inside of me let him hug me so hard that I'd cum without warning and how he'd cry with happiness like he knew I was about to cum (because he was already cumming too) and how he'd cry because he knew that the kind of love we had was the absolute worst kind of love (because it was real) and how

it was all a way to get nearer to the universe and to the elements that we were made out of: when the universe sparked and

when Time was slick with afterbirth

and yes death always enters into life and it entered into my life early and yes that first spring was wonderful when he and I made love like crazy every night and I didn't think about anything including how finite we really were and we never imagined that evenings faded or that things ended and I blame him for not acting his age (P was reading SUCH serious things in those days) and for putting me in place: telling me that I was foolish and idealistic when he was really the one who

and could have at least done something to put a damper on our expectations for the future: for my expectations that the difficulty of being a child in the household of my parents would go away permanently and that the esctatic aura of early-middle youth would not fade like an evening redness in the sky

telling myself not to get caught up in this

thinking that I haven't even fully gotten rid of THAT feeling

(having only buried it like I would bury a body outside the city walls)

and my father pulls me aside and says that long ago your mother and I were really in love and isn't she pretty?! my aunt exclaims from the kitchen

the geraniums (painted with moonlight) floating around us in and above the grass and the trees and the stars hanging from the tips of the sky and his mouth blooming with foam his body conducting mine into sorrow (love and death and dying) and how does it manage to fall like rain through our hands? (love) and how does it master us with darkness? (when it ends)

I would tell him to find somebody else (because I would panic) because I would think that I wasn't good enough wasn't decisive enough wasn't serious enough for him (the Poet) and I liked that he took me seriously and told me it was nonsense (my telling him to find someone else)

and I liked that he never changed his mind about that (that he never fell into the traps that I set for him) and that the only trap he fell into was never being cold enough to keep me close by

and now suddenly:

I am five years old looking down at my navel while my mother bathes me: I am attached to the universe there: at this place which marks my original entrance into the world like a scar

a reminder that to want something from pain is to exchange want for want: it is to go sideways

and that sacrament of pain: it is mine: it is everybody else's

and we said we would drive to the sea and never come back and we never did and that was a kind of end for us and a year later I was someone else and I told him I was getting married to Richard and that's how fast things go (as if we were skipping chapters in a novel) and everything we did was unintentional and everything we did had the grace of surprise

and to hell with that I thought: the casual fucking and the names we called each other and the promises we made without thinking

the things I said to him in that last letter (the letter I wrote the day I became engaged to Richard) were especially crushing because I knew him so well by that point that I could absolutely carve him to the joint: carve him any way I wanted

and it gives me such a bittersweet feeling knowing that the day he received my letter was the same day as the day we met

because it's the first swerve away (sex) from love:

and then you have the Greek idea that character is fate and that's true I think and comforting too in a way

because voices eyes hands lips have their own rhythm:

because I left him:

because women need men less than men need women:

and one night when my father is out and doesn't come home Melissa and I get drunk and Melissa takes off her shirt and lets me kiss her breasts which I kiss and kiss (because they're so exceptional)

*and I felt like my father kissing them (Melissa's breasts)
and I've always wondered since then what it would have
been like to have been with a woman instead of a man*

*giving into some kind of essential softness like running
one's hand underneath a pillow in between stages of a
dream*

*but love is love in the end: things come down to the same
desires and the same struggles (power need insecurity
akrasia)*

*and I used to have this image of my analyst as a giant
maggot who fed on everything that hurt me: a maggot
who grew larger and larger in size the more I was hurt*

*and of course I hated those appointments twice a week
because my mother made me take them like medicine
(the kind of medicine you take to keep you ill)*

*and when the body dies it looks bruised like a crab-apple
fallen on the ground and death pours in through the
breaches like wind through an open door*

*and soon enough the body (that rotting apple) is gone
completely returned to the earth for good*

and OK: YES:

*I feel enormous sadness at not being THERE all the time
(with him I mean) (P)*

37

because for a long time he was the only consistent thing in my life: the only thing that I lived for and in a way for the last thirty years he's continued to be what I live for (and he doesn't even know it doesn't even begin to realize that

(the quality of silence is organically linked to the quality of language)

and then there was my friend Katie who thought it was marvelous that I smoked cigarettes and 'fucked' and snuck out of the house and met actors downtown and got high and later I met Katie with her husband at Elaine's and the husband seemed like a kind of smarmy banker type but she seemed happy (but only the kind of happiness that people have who never get over being impressed by smoking and fucking and getting high)

but Katie and I were born into the same shitty generation in America: a generation that was given too much and not enough at the same time

so she should consider herself lucky to have found a nice stupid smarmy type to cling to and I bet she does (feel lucky) (even today)

because I understand that people have fenced themselves in with miles and miles of unexamined wonder

to the point where even the spectacle of beauty does not bring love to life limestone quarried from this cleft in memory: the limestone I'll use to build a house for the dead

and recalling already this evening the look of him from afar with the years bundled like twigs behind my back

the smile on his face while reading the same as it used to be (structurally/geometrically): like he is making a very funny joke to himself (a joke that no one will ever understand or find remotely funny)

and it would be like starting over without imagined roses (because his poems aren't worth anything I tell myself)

and of course they're worth more than I'm willing to admit (but I'll never admit it: I can't)

shame being a kind of self-regulation mechanism that pulls you into where you should be and makes it possible for you to live

and what do I see now? nothing really: the back of my hand pressed to the center of my forehead

because we had a method of suffering that was ingenious and highly-evolved

and if he turned around to look at me I said to myself that I'd disappear like the sun behind a glass building but he didn't so I didn't and I won't have to now and my god what bullshit this is: I need to stop but I won't because I like indulging these kinds of thoughts (I always have)

but today so rainy and grey and miserable generally and then seeing him? I don't know how I did it I never imagined I would have to go through THAT but then again it was my choice wasn't it? and no one really knows why they do anything in life do they? (and we shouldn't pretend otherwise)

and look at this: breasts sagging hair stiff like flax

and my hands (once smooth) are wrinkled and whiteish: the blood drained from them like amber from a tree

because a poem announces us to the sorrow we've forgotten: pins us to the butterfly wings of fate

and one night my mother locks me in my room until evening the next day and I only have a glass of water next to my nightstand

and I remember not really feeling anything not sleeping not doing anything not feeling concerned not feeling anything except afterwards having this almost physical reaction (hives breaking out across my back) and I'm not sure what my mother meant to accomplish by locking me in my room

maybe she was trying to kill me or create the illusion of killing at least (that must be it) and she never did anything physical she wasn't physical at all it was a kind of mental thing (wanting me to experience what she experienced on the inside)

but Mr. Matthews always knew the right things to say to me and my love letter wasn't sexual at all: it was pure appreciation

because I don't think anyone understood that a girl like me (minus a brother and really a father too my whole life) would just be grateful to talk to someone (a man) whom she respected

because Mr. Matthews spoke Latin and French and German and gave me Jane Austen and Dostoevsky and Melville and Emerson and Emily Dickinson and Goethe and took my education so seriously (and did I say that I didn't deserve him yet? because I didn't and I still don't)

because it was shame almost perpetual shame for me then beginning with my mother extending through everyone including P

and in a way my success hasn't ended that shame only covered it up like wallpaper over rot

and one thinks and thinks about these people who one hasn't seen in ages and I barely ate today just drank ten cups of green-tea and sat for an hour at my kitchen table rereading the newspaper thinking about those awful

*poems of his and how moving they were when spoken
aloud*

*and he when returns from the underworld (arms full of
flowers) will he recognize the light and air of my body
passing back through his eyes?*

*and does he remember the evening when he took my
virginity? when I bled on his kitchen floor while the dog
was scratching at the door and the sunlight around us
was getting warmer and warmer*

*and how funny it was: the blood and the sunlight and the
dog and our bodies broken like old bones*

*and even without eyes I'd still see him without a tongue
still taste him: still speak to him*

*and I'd place my body in the urn of him: regenerate my
body from his seed*

*because the two of us are like clouds passing into rain
sinking into earth (our souls knotted together like tree and
vine) and it was like he meant to remind me with his
poems that he hadn't forgotten me*

*or that some initial pattern still holds (our closeness our
forgiveness our openness)*

growing like a flower amongst the rocks (hidden)

and my thoughts begin to resemble a room filled with white moths to the point where one cannot see or even breathe

staggering all over downtown with a cigarette between my teeth thinking that THIS (THIS!) was thirty years gone down the drain

an entire cosmology of pain: a past a lifetime of physical sorrow

or like he says in one of his poems 'open a pellet of rain like a flowerbud: pour your voice inside its shell'

and for my teenage years he took priority over everything and to the detriment of everything and now someone would define that (my behavior) as a sign of addiction:

because he let me sleep on his bed all afternoon after school I was so incredibly tired most if not all of the time maybe because I never had any time to just be alone because there were always people asking for something from me even P (my lover) and just everyone everyone everyone wanting more than I could give

and if I had a daughter I would let her live in the mountains I'd let her wander through meadows braid the sunlight in her hair drink milk straight from the pail

be free from who I was from what I was from the unhappiness I suffered to please my parents:

my mother who sent me to a psychiatrist who suggested
a lithium dosage that would have meant a disruption of
my metabolism: sleep body temperature: mind body soul

and I knew girls even in those days at school who needed
something other than talk-therapy to keep them happy
(with their miserable old mothers breathing down their
necks) and I imagine it's only gotten a million times
worse for girls in New York City these days (I really
pity them I do) and if it wasn't for P I probably would
have started taking lithium and gotten my grades up and
generally been a good well-functioning Depressed Person
Just Like Yourself but thankfully I could say with pride
'thank you but no thank you Herr Doktor I'm being well-
fucked twice or thrice a day so I've got everything I need'

and there was dear Eliot (my mother's ritzy boyfriend)
who took me to the symphony and let me cry as much as
I wanted (because the music was so absolutely beautiful)
and we listened to the Cleveland Orchestra on the radio
on Tuesday nights and I liked Eliot (I really did) and
I wonder why he stayed with my mother all those years

(seeing how whole strands of my life are starting to weave
themselves together in me like bits of music (chords
melodies counterpoints leitmotifs))

because our love twists like the stems of flowers

the chord of grief: the blackest spring

my womb emptied my tongue unbound:

a nostalgia for simple happiness:

daisies in Central Park following the sun days disappearing like clouds and no we can't join them no we can't fall back

sitting at my kitchen table watching the remnants of the rain fall from space lazy and self-satisfied and it would be foolish to believe that suddenly (at my age) love could be simple

an emotion concealed so as to unconceal (like stars at night in the city) and

trying not to think of him anymore trying to find a reason to go start a conversation with Richard but not being able to do either stop thinking or start talking to Richard being stuck on THIS on HIM on P

like a branch split off from the living trunk

knowing that I'm removed from birth and death (the irrevocable human necessities) and was it mercy or cowardice? I wonder (leaving him for Richard)

because Love unshells us: spits us out unconsumed

and now I'm thinking of Antigone: the woman caught in the snare of Law and Love because every woman sacrifices herself beneath the city walls (only the city is always changing and the sacrifice is never the same)

life being just a demonstration of strength rather than an act of conviction or daring or anything lovely or

he comes in my mouth I swallow it (I swallow him): every drop a scrap of his language

and do I feel shame at fifteen? no I cannot feel shame with him: no not him: never him (I never will)

and right before the curtain went up on the school production of A Midsummer Night's Dream: there I was begging him to fuck me in the third floor school bathroom (where we wouldn't get caught but where it was not inconceivable that we would)

and whatever nervous emotions I had about the stage were inconsequential to what I wanted which was human closeness human warmth his seed between my thighs life running between us like an electric current (what acting continues to be for me) a tunnel-channel from here to Being: from him on through me into the ground the sky the trees the old island of Manhattan before the Dutch arrived the earth spinning roundly on its pin the sun shining (rebirth present in every hour of the day) deductions arrived at invisibly: my heart my soul my thoughts a cigarette a cup of tea Richard asleep early in the other room the script for the new play we mean to do together sitting on the sofa an email from our son printed out and slipped in between the script (for Richard to find) (my way of doing things) and what am I saying? that life has these two tracks one diverging from the other at all points (never converging) never arriving at the same destination but coming close close enough even to wave shout hello goodbye see you whenever and I always thought of my life as containing all these almost-infinite potentialities at once

because changing would mean admitting a failure an unhappiness a lie: and so we remain as we are: we interpret the past so that it remains presentable to us in memory

like the way butterflies dream of next year's wings: so obscene and lovely pulled apart in the hands

intimacy rooted in the earth: dormant touched by warm rain my feeling for him returning (like the volume is being turned up gradually in me)

nature asleep its eyelid shut like the door of a house on a quiet country lane

'for I must now to Oberon' I said for the first time and suddenly I had a Life in Art

a stringy sometimes beautiful girl then actress then wife then mother then actress-mother-wife in no particular order (actress-mother-wife: wife-actress-mother)

or simply Woman Proper Mother Proper Wife Proper: all of these things that identify themselves as Me

having never ceased being at heart (simply) the girl who panicked at everything the girl whose heart raced and whose hands shook for fear of people and their secrets

my anger at feeling that no one appreciated that I was essentially Good and that all I ever wanted was to GIVE and GIVE and GIVE

submissive and devouring (I was both)

remembering how his father would gather all kinds of people for great sessions of talk and alcohol and coffee and tobacco and how I would allow myself to linger and listen while P would look at his father half-proudly unsure if he could ever grow into this sort of life (this aesthetic well-furnished tweedy bohemian Brooklyn life) or if he had to become something else (something Rilkean and elegant and distant and foreign) and that is (in a way) what he became: a Rilke-type: looking for the female artist-lover (the soul-twin) that would complete him

and I know that I was a phase or staging-station from which he could launch himself into a deeper more masterful love with some OTHER higher being and

I was so jealous (have I said this already?) because I knew that I wasn't deep enough for him and that one day he would leave me leave for a woman who REALLY moved him and what a goddamn idiot I was believing that even if it WAS true (and who knows if it actually was) (obviously I'm still insecure)

and I wonder if he still smokes cigarettes and if I should've gone to the reading today and sacrificed myself at the altar of Him like I did when I was young

my soul conforming to his poetry at every level every orbit every disregarded state of being and today has been an atrocious and desperate and inconceivable day (the best day I could have hoped for)

and I don't want a life deprived of secrecy and quiet I want a life of a cozy rooms and hideaways

and imagine trying to drag that body over the daedal earth unsure of what lies ahead at dawn: the waking of Cleon: the thundering of the guards

like how I would wake P in the middle of the night and beg for him to fuck me wanting to give myself (my new hips and breasts) to him (hoping that he was as weak (as needy) as me)

a change: a lapsing away from him: his hands on my abdomen his teeth on my neck (on my bare body) wind-worn like silk under his fingertips when I would hold myself out to him and those were the loveliest the days after school with the arrivals and the goodbyes and later the visits in college and the closeness brought on by the time apart and the letters that we broke off only to see each other: as if It (the to-&-fro of the heart) was never ending

my father throwing a bottle at Melissa's head and Melissa throwing a bottle at his and me turning off the lights in the room screaming at both of them to stop

and all this was happening too at the same time (the severe trauma of my ordinary life) and falling in love (remember those two unconverging tracks?) and desperately I wanted to leave New York: desperately I wanted to be someone else (then as now)

listening to Sibelius' Fifth Symphony he pinned me to the floor and watched me cry and I think summer had begun by then and school was over and we had all day to ourselves but I'm not sure any more because the chronology is unclear

what I do know is that we threw away our kindness assuming it was useless

reaching out towards disintegration (whispered cries lips torn open by teeth: fingers prying open the anus-mouth) and oh how he went along with it how he took off his tie put down his classics his poetry his records his ethics all so that he could so beautifully abuse me

because I had dreams even then of being onstage and delivering his language like pure music (the stage-lights washing me clean)

my chest heaving underhand his mouth glued to mine his tongue

he was a cipher: a half-revealed form

because unsundered finally he was joined to me again at that point of arrival and we were going forward through dense waves of time and so I told myself that if the mirror arrives first you must look through it and I bought his new book and by tomorrow morning I'll have read it three times (despite myself)

and that was why he loved me (the symmetry of my inwardness) why he called me to him why he held me and loved me and stroked my forehead with his fingertips and why he disassociated himself from my sensuality (my paganism my indifference) my

because he had this stupid idea of himself as a future classics professor and poet (a man with a clean house full of books who had no room for a fucked-up girl with a prescription for lithium and parents who hurled furniture and plates across the room and a basketcase pathological sister who

the rain will dishevel us make us look gaunt and so
we are always blossoming in some land of the dead
(apophrades):

that is what I wanted to tell him today

when I was furious with my own father for not coming
to the school play   P and his father (who were there)
comforted me and said nice things about me and about
how good (how natural) of actress I was (how Puckish
how dazzling how full of spirit)

and yes from the graves of roses and the meadows of light
we got the idea (yes) that we should turn into trees like in
Ovid or like the fairies in Shakespeare and that was fine
with me (and that idea is still fine to me)

on cold spring mornings waking up together me sneaking
home on the subway dangerously at five a.m. thinking
about him: still feeling his lips on my skin

and those were the wounds of longings: those evenings
that lead to mornings

those spring evenings before summer nights

and everything after (our lives apart my marriage) still
renders me speechless with disappointment

and at sixteen I understood everything about sex that I
have forgotten now

because I put myself through it (trousered blue legs set apart his mouth his eyes his poems like smoke curling around the bookstore filling every nook)

because he was like no one else

being more like cobwebs or cigarette-ash

or like rain falling from a broken cloud

and fluttering through the city like a pigeon did he think I wanted to elude (evade) him just to let another decade pass? let another structure of time break off like an iceberg from the whole and float across the membrane of time? because no how could I? how could anyone?

and I don't want anything except that gorgeous interiority of his (his solipsism curling on top of my consciousness like the cream in a cup of milk)

because the lovely kiss themselves away in expectation and we know that the soul has a kind of endurance that we can't understand because we've so fully immersed ourselves in its suffering

when we use the future tenses (that mysterious capacity to talk about events concerning the morning after our death) we are excercising the part of language that makes us human (or so I remember P saying once in a moment of inspiration ((or something resembling inspiration))) and look at what is unconcealed: the grief of a mother mourning a child lost early (the abortion I had)

and as for those trios quartets quintets impromptus fantasies sonatas of longing? today I remembered them (I heard them) again

whole orchards of blue apples fading into the duskblue lamplight: images of the impossible the dreamlike the unknown the!

his eyes the sound of his voice the emotion that he must have seen obliquely in the way that I moved through the door all of this I still retain in my body like a charged current of light

poetry meshing itself with my secrets turning me back into who I was turning me back upon the whole matrix of birth disintegration death despair

speaking in that most enigmatic grammatical figure

our mouths pressed together blue and gluey our tongues pulped like old books his eyes open my eyes open

pale petals and dead nightingales: all that we grieve for

and we were willing to hurt and be hurt and that was Love

but it wasn't fair that he was older and had read more books and had BIG IDEAS about LIFE no it wasn't very fair that he let me sense that he wouldn't be content forever with living in the shade of Brooklyn teaching at a small college having a wife like me to come home and fuck twice a night for the rest of his life but these were always my projections my neurotic renderings of everything he said (and he never said that he wouldn't discover how small I was and how pathetic: never assured me on that point) and even after I became successful in the theater I never felt like I deserved him or anything he ever did for me (love me) or anything his father ever did for me (talk to me kindly) and maybe that's why you know I ended up with Richard but that seems too obvious or too reductive or both

a fate maybe one thinks of it like that (like Fate) but it isn't fate so much as it is self-control

my success being only a byproduct of the charisma P transferred to me on top of what little I inherited from my father (that drunken Slavic charm)

our laughter not like the fruit of innocence but the seed

and then the next year being sent to boarding school (oh god: boarding school) thanks to my mother and Eliot's ability to write a check for some ungodly sum that was the beginning of things-falling-apart though it would take awhile with the hiccups and the false-start-endings and everything else our sex always being more than a fuck because I never could help it (loving him)

it's like magic we agreed: knowing that it will end (life) (and music too) (the music inside of us and everything outside of us too) (the stars)

and how easy it is to be strong in this world and how difficult to be weak and he was never anything more than a prism for seeing myself I think

and I won't call him or send him an email just yet (I'll listen to the rain and think about how this was or how this wasn't and how today felt like the end of something that has been rising and falling within us for ages and ages)

half-husked (the erotic flower)

now at the end of the first movement of our last phase the music sweeping us forward over the first bar towards the final

?

my father fails to understand why I wanted him to come to my play and why such details mattered to me (specifically his being there) and why any daughter needs something SOMETHING more than just a wavering unsteady presence in the background of her life (ignoring the fact of what he did to my mother) and in the grand scheme of things this is why I don't bother taking my damned lithium and why Melissa isn't right for my father and why my sister is a bitch and why my mother is a bitch and why I lie to everyone about where I sleep and why I'm so happy/unhappy all the time (why all of this matters or doesn't): because it would have been nice if he had just even sat through to the intermission in order to see me deliver a few lines (his father's daughter) and:

traceless the future of nothing (our solitude) two distant things

goosedown from the mattress floating like clouds pulled apart in the sunlight after making love and P laughing to himself and me not wanting to be reduced to necessity like that (because what I want is the utmost of my own freedom)

unconscious of the bloom his body roughly against mine singing

veronica jasmine broken glass of a milk bottle and a reading from Sappho on the roof

because everyone in the Village loved my father and because he had real talent (unlike my mother) even if he wasted it

and because each thing seems a separate whole: P: my father: my husband: my son:

my house built on trembling unstable soil

and each thing becomes enrolled in this music

becomes a voice like the kind we make narratives out of

(these voices evolving like the wind)

and to be unhappy is to think about one's parents and I will not be unhappy I swear

sunlight breaking around my body seeping through the pores of my skin (the sexual orchid blooming) the light flowing through my hair through his hands flowing across the bed and 'use me' I beg him 'use me' (and he uses me)

and later I become a person who lives for the way other people change when she's in the room

and I only knew how jealous my sister Clara really was of me (over P) after she told me that SHE was the one who wrote that letter to the school telling them those horrible untrue things about me and Mr. Matthews (that caused Mr. Matthews to resign suddenly at the end of the year)

and I have a kind of permanent anger and disappointment with human beings (with the people I am supposed to love) and what does it mean that a teacher like Mr. Matthews has to quit his job because he is somewhat handsome and because his students like him? or that some of the worst teachers I ever had taught until they

*were 83 (probably) getting more inflexible and stupid
with every year*

*(it means that a tremendous flux is already flowing away
in every direction that moments of time are already
waiting for us to feel their presence and that life is not an
exercise but an EVENT of circumstantial unimportance
and unmet desires and random occurrences and random
acts of emotional violence that we can't account for)*

*so we must take our love up again like it was always
there*

*because time voided gushes forward into a vacuum
(opening) and by another man (my husband) I have a
child named Julian who is 25 (who I've formed around
like a tree: each ring of him sacred within me) who lives
in Seattle Washington and writes software code and who
has a girlfriend and lives in a nice apartment and who
calls his mother twice a week and who sends his mother
pictures over email of him and his girlfriend and their
dog hiking somewhere and who seems absolved of the
pathos of his mother (which is a good thing) even if for
some reason she regrets it (that her son is someone she
doesn't recognize)*

*and CHRIST how tired P must be of book-parties and
listening to less talented writers quote from their memoirs
and complain about teaching duties and all that (the cost
of maintaining a home in Sag Harbor et cetera et cetera)*

because I liked watching his father drink whiskey with his writer friends in that wonderful old home in Brooklyn the rain coming down in sheets and not feeling obligated to saying anything at all

this being an analogy for what's been lost

and the ground opens: flowers spin up: sunlight lands on the paving stones

and in my son my existence has real shape

(not like this threadbare thing: my body)

and we're going to bloom again in the spring flourish in the summer decay in the fall die in winter because that's what people do (P and I): because contradictions are facts

and beauty is crippling for a girl especially when she realizes that she has it (and I had it)

and it must have been on Waverly and 11th that I saw him walking with his wife or thought I did (a few months before 9/11) and I ran away as fast as I could and thinking about it now I realize it was probably someone else

and I'm thinking: 'he must feel the same for me he must not have forgotten' because his books are books of disquietude (and yes) the enchantment is always there (but always a little less each day each year)

and strangely after I left him for Richard I never took lithium again (or any other kind drug for that matter) and never felt the need and I wonder

because he wanted a beautiful soul (that's what he told me) and he said it was me (obviously) who had IT (that beautiful soul) and my god how astonishing that was to hear (and how wonderful)

no I explain it away because I can't conceive of so isolated a consciousness: as purely cold and desireless as Richard's seems to me (and always has)

but there remains an equation to be worked out: the relative value of being boring about being interesting: of being interesting about being boring: of living just to keep alive like I have (given the instability of memory and its changing nature and the loss of energy leaping from present to past continually)

and yes yes my universe is erotic (seeking completion)

and no: for historical biological/genetic aesthetic theological philosophical reasons I can't imagine that any fully functioning human organism could forget about love (especially me) although if we can't forget it we can abandon it like a broken-down car along the highyway

and now re-staging something that is inside of me like a matinee on a rainy day

and reading his poems I think (despite myself) that his feeling is as great as ever that he still longs for me and the understanding we had and

but then there is Richard: a decent man who is generally unastonished by the evolution of life around him

Richard who sees no terror in nothingness

Richard to whom saying no to would be like saying no to a child

and it's fair to say that my father's selfishness meant that for the rest of my life I never really trusted anyone except for Julian

but you can't reduce anyone to anything: human beings are deeper than that: we are like trees and rivers and stars and suns

love passing through hatred like the sun through the clouds

joy vanishing before silence my inner life now flowing out of him and his poems (this spring is the perpetual spring of bone marrow and blood) and I needed so much to be

*loved and recognized by him and when I was younger I
was afraid of what I had to give to him but now?*

*sliding his tongue around my mouth placing his hands on
my hips after running inside from the rain stripping me
clean kissing me on the stairs my chest trembling with
happiness I said I loved him and I meant it*

*and it will bring us down to our creatureliness our sadness
our sorrow our finality (and 'don't leave me now don't
ever leave me' I want to cry to no one in particular)*

*the earth resembling the human body (its rivers its
mountains its plains) but this doesn't mean that it dies
like us or dies the same*

*Richard and I living together (like we are burying a
body)*

writing an anthropology of silence

*watching cloudlets of unfallen rain: three stones to stone
the heart: the almost nightblack evening deepening
around my apartment Richard snoring in the other room
a text message from Julian asking how I'm doing (just
OK)*

*and I still have questions about why nature cycles
through us and why we arrive again at who we were
and why the sound of an accordion is tactile and why I
am tactile and why the sun is tactile and why the rain*

is tactile and why the wind is tactile and why I'm here now remembering everything without being able to stop stop stop stop stop

these emotions like sunlight soaking through a stone

and as I remember it: years pass I leave for school P attends Columbia for graduate school I come back we lay on his apartment floor (now in Harlem) we go to coffeeshops sit for hours read books exchange sweaters talk about nothing (about philosophers playwrights poets pornographers politicians) go back to his apartment lay on the floor wait for the heat to come on talk about ourselves (my self-immolation his distance my depression his silence my contradictions his art our sex our desire our hopelessness our

(and it all makes sense when I step away from myself: watch myself grow out of the ground like a tree)

but no I shouldn't skip ahead too fast and why? because I

nothing else to do but make love and drink bad coffee and mill around bookstores and go to movies and use New York City like a staff to fill up with our notes of longing

realizing that I only began to masturbate after I left him for Richard and after I had gotten married and I don't think I've ever made the connection until now even though it was so obvious (but that's how the mind works arranging its material in anagrams for later deciphering) and as for the fact that we let the air out of spring? that we let the body become a thing perpetually at the point of crisis?

(I can't say)

so I begin to resemble a tree stripped of its leaves

like the second half of a double-helix winding its way up the spine of his books: the memory of me

it caused me so much pain to read those his published poems because no one ever began to replace him and because no one has ever wasted the largest of love so easily as we did (as I did)

the unsung part of the verse like spring unflowered in me:

we'll undress ourselves and remember how much (how beautifully) we've suffered and how we'll dissipate when the night falls (when the rejected chapters assert their place in the order of our being)

all mixed up now an affection for life struggling to take wing

reading in the paper that his father died was worse than when my own parents died much worse and worse than when my sister died of cancer

and time projects itself across the screen of life and everything (roses bending one by one) suddenly disappears and a regret is just one of those things a person has to learn to love (like a poem)

the last daylight shifting imperceptibly back and forth across my apartment

because Julian is the one barrier between my old life and the life I've made permanent (my life with Richard and our successful life together and our success onstage and our apartment and our infidelities)

unharrowing darkness between the rooms my mother making tea wiping her hands on her apron playing Chopin on the piano in Eliot's apartment my mother crying and Eliot comforting her not knowing why she's crying

my mother who keeps clippings of old theater reviews my mother who curses outloud having read that my father has opened a successful new play

that my father is the toast of the town et cetera et cetera

because that he (my father) is happy and she (my mother) is sad and he (my father) is in love and she (my mother) is not and he (my father) lives with a younger woman who is more beautiful than she (my mother) is and that that will never change (the inferiority of her charm)

the enigma of selflove being proof that somehow the love he gave me was unlike any other love (a love that we exchanged like flowers)

*driving out to Lake George in his father's car talking
about movies (Max Von Sydow Mastroianni Monica
Vitti and so on how we'd move to Italy or Sweden and
how he'd write a book that would become a movie) and
about politics sports (he loved baseball) and the poets he
had met (on the subway in Union Square in Chinatown
in The Strand in Central Park in Queens on the Metro
North in Jersey City at Brooklyn College at NYU) the
poets he wanted to be (Shakespeare Keats Whitman
Rilke Crane Neruda Stevens Ashbery) and the poets he
wanted to become (himself)*

*because he sank his fingers into me watched my torso
crumble around him like a falling tower and making love
was wildly vibrant because it was like we had one nature
and purpose (and it's a miracle to be alive I think it's*

*the sun running across a brook throwing itself over my
naked body and how beautiful those black clouds looked
foisting themselves up over us and how strange a bird's
white feathers seemed falling like snow from the trees*

*knowing that a memory is a projection (which sticks to
our hands like glue) connecting us to everything living
thing (the whole diffusion of people across the universe)*

*my thighs wet my hair pulled back my mouth open (my
unkindness my sex) returning guiltlessly to him having
given him everything having lain with him amongst the
rushes crying*

the centrifuge being something else something more radiant than what we understand and I won't call it nature but I won't call it God either and to P I want to say 'kiss me on the cunt open my lips to your hands turn my inner-thigh out let your tongue slip along my hipbone let our bodies grieve for each other finally Peter yes'

and I never could prefer Eliot to my actual father because I've never prefered people who are kind to me to those who are cruel

now sifting through old thoughts old letters old sensations at the kitchen table with my husband napping afraid to come to the conclusion that tragedy or Fate or any other metaphysical idea governs us during the course of our lives

a swoon a fallen blossom a mirage made of desire that button hook and laces unravels softly in my hands before a rough fuck in the back of a car his fingers curled into my guts figments of lungs lips hands like wheat buds rough against my eyes the light at the magic hour like mud spread across a piece of white paper

and loving a person means attaching yourself to a spot of time you shared with them and refusing to leave

like in the slow movement of Mahler's 5th in Central Park and it was so painful to be around him (even him) with music like THAT going and what I'm talking about is a deafness in the music that heard ME

like a first and then less subtle death: seeing him again no longer like the man he was and we dared fate to wreck us today (and it (FATE) wrecked ME at least)

tongueless songs beautiful and useless like dreams are

because one must take these rich magical days: polish them like silver

and years later I found Mr. Matthews teaching Latin at some Catholic school out in the middle nowhere and I thanked him profusely and gave him a ticket to one of my plays and though he didn't come I was still happy knowing that he was OK because I owed him something (because I still needed to say a simple 'thank you' or 'I appreciated everything you did')

because it wasn't Mr. Matthew's fault that other people suspected him of being too close to his students or something like that no it was our fault it was the fault of the constrained and still moralistic strain of Old New York that I hated so much then and still do

fluttering back like a bird to the nest of emptiness I've made for myself: the thoughts (the logic) of P (P and ~P) and I and the poetry he wrote that was a symbol for something even more ALIVE than us

almost at the last memory now of that spring surfacing
slightly of him painting me laying in a beach chair on his
roof and I never told him how clear-headed I felt sitting
in that beach chair not moving so that he could paint me
and I never should have never moved from that chair
and I never should have grown up and become an actress
or gotten married or had a child or grown old

the ridiculous things he wanted to be then: Aristotle
Wallace Stevens Lord Byron Hemingway Fitzgerald
Joyce Stravinsky Bob Dylan Kierkegaard Picasso
Rembrandt Rousseau Hart Crane Thoreau his father
Saul Bellow Iris Murdoch Woody Allen Leonard Cohen
Groucho Marx

tangles of tangles of tangles (saliva and dirt): the
transparence laid over the clarity of ordinary days: over
everything and I don't wanna think about my life now
(with the adagio coming on) because I know that when I
see myself I'll look almost like an old woman (closer and
closer to an old woman than what I ever was)

because a body must bear itself out of nature like a
newborn bird crying for silence

because then I begin to realize that what is between me
and other people isn't kinship but a kind of a gulf (or gap)
that flows like electricity across a body of water

and at the lake we want nothing else other than to be where we are and I mail absurd letters to my parents along with a letter to my sister informing her that I will never speak to her again (and I never do) and for awhile we sit on the sand and smoke cigarettes and contemplate our freedom and he talks about Rilke and Lou and what it must have been like with two people like that or like Antonioni and Monica Vitti or Mastroianni and Sophia Loren or Godard and Anna Karina and we watch the evening sun wash over the lake and I feel his absence thread through me like a needle

because I'm trying to isolate this FEELING that has moved me my whole life: this desire to LIVE and not to die

though I never told him that I also fell deeply in love with a girl who was in my English class but who wouldn't have anything to do with me (the year I met him) (right before I met him in fact) and not that I think about it I never told anyone and there are so many feelings like that which never were allowed to become a part of the narrative

and what life requires we give (that we diffuse ourselves across the membrane of hope)

because beauty is a ghost (the dogrose and the spring all done for) and unconsciously my body floats and spreads itself across the water of his heart beating under my skin and the sun leaks out of the clouds and I kiss him on the cheek and he returns my kiss and he runs his hand behind my neck and tells me that he wants to strip me to the bone

because he always had a note of childishness and sophistication which struck an answering chord in me

and I smooth it out (this ripple of existence):

unravel my thrushsong: my innervoice

and we smoke cigarettes as the sun sets and we open a wine bottle on the sand and THEN: this astonishing thing called happiness

a whole universe we created for ourselves: a bare (radiant) vowel of love: the difference between us and others and the dead: silent/unsilent under a thick wave of time: shining/unshining

the muscle of sound carving desire into a new kind of mourning

tensed like an animal ready for violence

and again I'm back in the experience-itself: seeing him standing naked in the doorway toying with his hair looking at me on the bed trying to catch my breath my hand on my chest heaving up and down up and down up and down because WE (the spiritually ungifted) develop our pain from within

because we are a part of something that we are barely aware of and because our presence is something beautiful and immense and because we are infinite and because we are a part of something that is infinite (and cruel) and because we'll go then with this grave music (ich muss sein like Beethoven said)

taking myself for drowned on the riverbank my hair tangled in my hands my lungs contracted his voice in my ear telling me that I am alive

given that stories are costumes that we try on it's important to know that when we pause our story we're naked and that we can know ourselves in another way (and stories can also be straightjackets and corsets and hobble skirts and foot bindings)

and the gesture of bearing a child was the gesture that created the possibility of continued life and meant the end of Ours

asphodels (wildflowers) (blue as any image plucked from the sea) in our hair

because we have this death-love in us that we carry forward through time: that we drag across the earth like a mattress stuffed with swandown and stones and what I felt that day by the lake or any day in New York with him was the love of God moving through me and under my feet vibrating musically between my fingers:

because beauty only throws us back on our own dimensions shows us our own secrets our own concealed images and P resented other people for not being like him and I resented people for not being kinder to me and P for seeing me more and more as an object for His Pleasure: as a part of his little network of beautiful things (paintings films books letters) rather than as a stringy girl with black hair and big eyes and big lips and hope hope hope for a future she can barely understand

pillars of roses falling gorgeously over the softness of cotton soaked through with sweat (his sweat) and his mouth tastes like coffee-and-oranges and this emerging bloom of feeling is like nature become aware of our presence within it (and it is bittersweet (our love)) and he says that I have my own gravity and he says that I am completely his and I do not believe him even though I do believe him and here again is the old panic (always the old panic that I am not good enough to be loved)

and across the ocean and across the sky and across the grain-fields he shouts 'I love you' and everything dances and sheds its outer layer and dissolves into the universe around us while he goes on shouting love love love I love you

this being the blood the sex the fracture of another self

a cab outside slowing down in the rain skids and here suddenly: a stop to everything: this unchoreographed emotion: my thoughts my thoughts about his thoughts our movement down the river of time:

New York and my family and his father and my school and his poetry (and everyone we ever knew and everything we ever did and

when my sister died I didn't go to the funeral and when my mother died I sat in the back of the church and when my father died I gave the eulogy and none of it was justified all of it was the wrong thing to do and I've never wanted to be anywhere so much as I wanted to be at that bookstore today listening to him read

like a Swiss army knife switching from past to present and back again: each mode a different way to whittle a stick or open a can

and the sadness of seeing him was the sadness of remembering myself (because of course it was)

so plunge into another discovery (it offers nothing) plunge again (surrender)

*flat on my back my hands crushing his head to my breast
my mouth open gasping for air*

a living image like a last quartet

*and I've never understood how life coheres or how I can
account for love on one hand and everything else on the
other and why I'm in a marriage with someone I resent
or why I've been so good at keeping things completely
separate (building different machines for different tasks
and different processes and allowing each system to
work independently allowing my life to work almost
automatically without my input as if it were only a world
I built and then stepped away from)*

*(a world that I intrude on only long enough to set things
in order before retreating back inside)*

*two voices and two voices singing independently of the
song*

(two voices searching out the

parlando andava per non parer fievole

*bluedusknight of the evening and absentee-roses and I
wait and wait and wait*

*everything vanishing into sweetness the strawberries and
dandelions bloom/unblooming in our hands having failed
to stay ourselves in time like two rocks adrift in space out*

of orbit his cabbage green eyes (his mea culpa) and so I opened my mouth and he filled it with his tongue (so long ago) and we had our first kiss and I still remember it exactly how it was

and after years of change and suffering I became the woman I am (obscure: no later: no light) and I remember what he said: that the present is eternal (two oceans of time enclosing two people side by side sub specie aeternitatis)

and a last memory now of making love on the roof as the sun is going down the question open between us whether this (this perfection) will last

and I could've cried to see him today at the podium the skin around his eyes mostly broken with age his mouth half-smiling knowing that maybe I wasn't the person that he remembered either that

a murmur of stones: the final gloaming:

II. Allegro

*like the surface of glass (having sat down to write you a
long perhaps very long email all that I can think about is
Brahms) isn't that*

*watching the snow deer pass through the backyard
watching the steam from my teacup trail after itself like a
ladder built rung by rung into the air*

*because I don't know what it was about seeing you Peter
but I think it had to do with knowing that I've been the
subject matter for a few major poetry books and that you
have a wife (who may or may not know who I am) and
that you wrote down your email address in my copy of
your book when you signed it (hoping I'd*

*and did you really think I'd come knocking on your door
like I was in the eleventh grade again (that I'd show up
out of thin air?): that you could restore the old habit of
afternoon screwing with a stroke of the pen?*

*because I'd like to give you the benefit of the doubt here
Peter I would but then again since the day I saw you
I've been divorced or close to it (literally: I filed for the
papers the next day) and Richard's reaction was not like
I expected (more angry than sad) and my son Julian did
not react at all because I don't believe he cares*

*and because people are only who they wish themselves to
be and we both know that to be true Peter (because that
was one of the lessons we taught each other among the*

many other painful-to-accept lessons concerning human understanding)

and each morning I wonder at the sun on my feet and my eyes open and the light I receive within me

and I've been waiting to hear from you (shamelessly) since the reading last spring but shamefully you haven't written so here I am and yes actual letters would be too painful but this is the best I can do (email) and I have no idea if you'll write me back because you have this ridiculous habit of being enigmatic and I wish you wouldn't be so enigmatic but you are and I haven't even begun this email because I'm feeling so ill-at-ease: so instead I'm just thinking it out like a mathematics problem in my head

and not a word of sorrow but what we bear within us and what rises in the midmorning light but the hymn of the past? and the sight of our old fearless selves walking through the snow? and I can't remember a winter morning as full of bitterness and grace as this one and I wonder what you listen to now Peter (because music used to be so important to you)

but now: no more shielding myself from scorn

inside of the emptiness of my house I feel

we shatter our voices: we feel as if we had smashed a violin against a tree: plucked the strings out with our fingers because of the utter human inability to transport the soul where it is needed (so the answer is that it's bullshit to use the word distance as opposed to what I meant in the first place Peter but I guess it's not fair to assume what you're going to say) and I reread every single poem in every single one of those slimblue volumes of yours again this winter and Peter I always knew you were the most gifted man I would ever meet and it was almost shameful to have wanted to possess you the way I have

belief conviction experience the decision the sudden whatever it is that cries out at the moment one breaks one's heart and I don't believe you fully understand your own capabilities because surely if you did you'd have recognised that I wanted you to cut into me you so deeply that I'd never recover (never love anyone else) and when I said I was leaving you for Richard I gave you the chance but you missed it

hence why I never tried to pin you down hence why I'd rather wonder about you than know you hence why I had that episode on the train that day a year ago

each morning for years each of us together rising singing loving (such sweet nonsense gabbering at nothing)

on the stage it would be much better if nothing happened (if the actors and actresses would be really there on the stage with their own lives the weight of THE PERSON (their presence and the weight of their lives)): that means very much to me and and the words you brushed once through my hair fall now like snowflakes in memory

and we avoid naming because naming would ruin us completely and It is something else (the way we talk about it): a kind of living disquietude but then again I'm not really speaking to you at all am I? (I'm only addressing you as I imagine you to be)

it's a vanquishing (an attempt at a vanquishing) a misguided backward devastatingly ill-fated attempt but an attempt and when I say empathy is everywhere it's everywhere it's in detritus and that's all I need: you know the expression of loving something to death? no you love it to life and that's my consolation you can't conceive of living without desire or intimacy because you have to explain it all away with theories of self-denial or religion or some type of deep-seated dormancy and is life outside of human relationships meaningless and frightening for you? Peter do you cultivate them merely to stave off your own fear of

the forever we couldn't have and your visits to me when I was in college? do you remember those? my meeting you on the train platform with gloves on my hands and the cold air slowing our lips down almost so that it was as if we were swimming?

and it comes apart in the hands (spiritual love) Peter it breaks apart: runs like eggyolk down our arms and I find everything about them moving (the flowers that grow like miracles in the winter): especially the way they are held in the hands of the girl I was and the everydayness of them (how they are plucked and severed from their source) and they are like people I think (plucked from emptiness) and it seems so purely pictorial at first (these images) but the poetry of them is drawn from something much deeper and you must know this Peter (you must be able to see what I see) and look!

and maybe the only difference between you and I was that you internalized your own bullshit and I didn't (that you wrote poetry and I auditioned for plays) and I needed someone to talk to as much as you needed someone to fuck and I was just happy to have you next to me while you internalized your own being-there and maybe we were only happy because for a few years Peter we perfectly fulfilled each other's need to conceal and disclose respectively what we really were to each other

and I'll hold back these thoughts (which are just like dreams really) until my lungs are ribbons and even then you'll see me flinging icicle arrows over the shoulder of death and the sex between us was too violent in its concreteness to be believed Peter it really was and I'll pass again into the cold and the white flowers of time will start to grow and we will say that we are neither living nor dead

(this is what no one talks about anymore: this beautiful annihilation)

my dining room table is covered in books and teacups but I'll keep from caring: so pin me to the walls again drape me over the chairs

swinging into the winter light my perception exfoliating the tongue stapled to the roof of the mouth and I could fan your petals for excess flame I could renew you in secret I could join you meddle in your heart (bind your movements to my eyes) because you are not without meaningful circumstances in your life the way I am Peter

limited in scope and pertinence (my analysis of why I did what I did but then again you never understood women in their absolute complexity because that kind of understanding wasn't necessary for your art was it?)

but only inhuman detachment would free us now I think or maybe it would not freedom never having been our true intent and it haunts us (the nature of the phenomenon) I think and we are all out of complications because we are always out of complications and during the winters we never left your house and naked against the floorboards you'd crush me and I would feel how cold your skin was and I would comb back the hair falling wildly over your eyes and nothing was bleak nothing was frozen-over (no not with the fire we had in us then)

Peter Peter Peter I can't believe that I'm considering writing to you now: because it seems so short

days enclosed by sunsets sunrises cold suns cold minutes my shadow halfway across the floor our longings seeping like water from ice or snow and Peter would you believe me enough to believe that I was leading a desperately interior life when you met me and lead me out of myself like the sun leads the moon out from behind the clouds

and there are secrets from these years I would never share: they are too intimate (in their bitterness) even for you and I'll say this to you: you have forced me to become someone else and it might have been a man I met waiting in the dentist's office or one of Richard's friends or a stranger in a motel room or god knows who else Peter anyone but you but it WAS YOU and you haunted me for so long (do you know that?) which is why I must must must must write to you in this obsessional run-on voice (the voice that I question even the reality of) and look at Time rising like Love Peter look at the morning sun (it's almost unimaginable) and do you remember when we said we were the kin of the stars? Peter? because we were so wrong we

(and it begins to feel like an eternity inside a fractal since I was close to you) and it's amazing to realize how one stores years of touch and intuition and (unreal) depth and how it only takes a second to let those things spill

like grain from within and I want to tell you something now that's very important to me but which I'm having trouble doing Peter I'm having so much trouble because I've hidden myself Peter I've

and it's only the very very important tropes that matter in a lifetime (friendship truth forgiveness hope) not the incidental ones (sex desire possession)

watch the air stir with music and shut your violence inside the clouds:

and look how I curl around my own tongue Peter: it's enough to stop traffic in the street (because people don't say who they are anymore: whether they're indifferent or whether they're a vessel of pain)

because I slipped through you into some other life when I married Richard

(since I let love pillar itself into salt)

and Peter I am still busy with your life and do you really think I only read 'The Dancer' just once Peter? because my god I read that book to pieces I read it until I physically couldn't turn the pages anymore (all because I knew that you wrote it for me and about me)

and once I remembered you stood up to my mother told her I was better than she was that she was jealous of me and that's why she was harassing us not giving us any privacy and that was the proudest I've ever been of someone (when you did that for me)

and what would you have me write to you Peter? that I'm still in love you with (bullshit) or that I want to still be in love with you (not-bullshit)

and you were always better at understanding my feelings than I was: that was your gift and my gift was simply being there for you to use as you like sexual rag doll et cetera because I was the plum or the lemon or the orange on the vice machine... I'm being indirect but surely you understand that (the indirection of language or symbols) and my god if only you'd break for me like I always broke for you (just once) and I'm coming back to a point here (the point that I just can't seem to get to)

and so far it's been impossible for you to forgive me yes it's been impossible (but it's possible too) and will you forgive me Peter? will you please? (forgive me?) please Peter you

and I'd cry and I'd feel so close to you and we'd read Beckett and talk about our parents getting old and about us getting old and how the unbarren unworn earth would dry up and how like suns we'd burn up split apart for good (fall like ash from the clouds)

and stillborn we come into life: bone and flesh quivering

and I would never never never admit to my son what happened between us (never) and the richness of these moments (these unbelievable events) depends on their being embedded in a certain kind of life a certain kind of emotional context (a context which I realize we have) and it was Winterreise you said into which Schubert distilled the sorrow of the world (the music which is part of that context of ours)

these old words are still in my blood somehow (I cannot annihilate them)

this being the fiction of having emerged from somewhere more perfect than where one is going

and believe it or not I've been damned happy without you and it wasn't my fault that I couldn't trust you no it was my parent's fault (and you must believe that can you please believe that?)

as if I am dropping into some dimness: into some time before I was myself

nothing but noise and we were cruel but I've always wanted you more than anyone else and you wanted to drag me out of this life into your art your poems your secrets and you're still married Peter (your fingers sliding up my chest peeling off my shirt moving the lips of my cunt apart does that ring any bells for you?) and reading your poems again I

but I couldn't it was too much so I simply stopped (but then again it's my throat darkened my eyes wide-open it's the music the presence that a person leaves that matters isn't it?)

fragile: just in full cry: the wind dying down

and you were perfect the way you were Peter (yelling from the floor shouting at me to turn off the record) you were somebody who seemed like they were always rolling out of bed at two in the afternoon so disheveled that they were always more alive than everybody else

pearl-pale: the image of you doing sit-ups on the floor as the sun is coming up

and my fingers flutter higher and higher and then down again white notes forming unforming in the air

as if in a silence that cannot be pierced like a protective shell and can you explain what we were protecting in ourselves by remaining together past the point of first excitement? (what unsayable thing what pointed understanding of what remained within)

(a recently divorced woman with a grown up son who is currently playing Irina Arkadina in a Broadway production of The Seagull) I wrote to you after my father died (remembering the starkness of your hands the crater of your mouth) and there was so much sorrow in that letter that

and all winter I waited all winter all morning all day Peter I waited I'm waiting I wait

but don't think for a second that within myself I am anything other than whole without you because I've found other ways to form myself I've found modes outside of your hungry stare

but I've the courage I do and you must believe me that's what gives life it's awful meaning

and we can talk about the Big Questions all you want Peter but it's just an evasion of the essential and essentially small question of moral commitment to another human being

intelligence in someone else (yes You) is enough to make me run for the hills and I've been running for a long time but I would like not to run anymore no I'd like to let you catch up (if you'd like to catch up)

winter stars wearing the skin of the sun turned insideout

stripping of individual words to their radical bones: an instrument wholly fitted to its excoriating purpose

both in constant expectation of the fulfillment of that sentence and in defiance of it

like the winter after 9/11 when Richard was suicidal and had to be hospitalized and I was strangely OK even though we knew people who

still wanting (I'm still wanting) poetry (your poetry) to redress the enterprise of living

because you were always reading at least five books (probably more) and you were a very difficult person to ever keep track of (the kind of cat who drags a dead mouse to display at your feet) except in your case the dead mouse would be a new writer a new language a new thought

and you really believed that something terrible happened to you when you met me (emotionally sexually artistically) and I think I got in the way of what you imagined your life to be (a married man a classics professor a classics professor who published poetry a man who had affairs with younger woman)

I mean Richard has ideas about what to do onstage but he is clueless about life (and his plays are mere tricks) but you know that already Peter you know it too well even if you've never had the opportunity to say it to me

because there was this dual going on between the psychologist in you and the sensualist (and remember how you described your own consciousness as a constantly-being-written novel of Dostoevski's?)

and you've not resolved that tension yet: that I could tell by just looking at you last spring but you aren't the kind of person who changes: you only ripen and ripen and eventually rot

and it's neither surprising nor ironic that I'm playing an aging woman who knows that her charms are up or will be sooner rather than later she'll be yanked off stage still crying to be seen and heard (that her experience will mean nothing when put up against the youth of another woman)

our despair our sonata our

because there are always these chords unpromised by birds unheard and there's always the feeling of you still there lingering on my skin (your hair your sex your sweat your mouth and everything whites and reds and yellows and blues) and you are as sweet as anything (the taste of violets and oranges fresh linens and warm tea: the life that I've constructed in the place of you) and all this (the memory of sweetness Peter) seems so cruelly distant midwinter with Winterreise in the background (I've changed the Brahms) and

I'd somehow managed to entangle the idea of being an actress with some notion of immunity from all future pain so when my mother died that fantasy was destroyed and I was left very lost for a very long time after quite possibly because I had never loved her

and when someone dies who you failed to love (and who never loved you in return) the bitterness is much greater than when someone you actually cared about passes

turning you into a bit of clay (turning you around in my hands) massaging the finer points of You into mannerisms that I can describe You by

and I did crazy things said crazy things because you were the only person in the world who really cared about me and because I was absolutely crazy about you

it was something that we dislocated ourselves from our light and sadness: that (immense) wave of everything radiant inside of us (everything we held open to each other like candles floating in the palms of our hands)

like the snow that enclosed us that kept us inside for days together we were fearless and we didn't need anyone and we didn't want anyone: we wanted each other only each other we only wanted

and you saw my openness as beautiful and

I remember how much you liked the idea of there being this friendly chubby little Viennese man who had many friends and no success and who was a pure source of melody:

Schubert being the perfect bourgeois artist (unconscious of how little he fits in with the bourgeois (which of course is exactly how you are))

and I disagree about mysticism I think it's unmanly I really do Peter it prevents us from taking in all the full meaninglessness of our human endowment (that's just my inner-Chekhov speaking for a moment)

and the answer is yes: it was terrible how we ruined it

because I'd ask to be buried in the earth and forgotten: grow later as a lily plucked by a child's fingers

and you shouldn't think for a moment that I've changed either (because it's about time for us both to admit that I'm more like you than we ever imagined)

and from nowhere it never ceased inside of me the sunlight the music of you the unmuted silence of everything the chrysalis of snow that mood of

brained ourselves in the dark broke open our love let it spill everywhere like moonshine

Django in the mornings: dancing around the kitchen you in your underwear with your hair half-covering your eyes yes I remember

and yes Peter you seized upon me pulled me down with words at least it always seemed so and I was so fond of you and so I gave in: decided to write to you again

a spider crawls up my wrist: draws my blood with its teeth

because I need to remind myself that what I'm really doing is waiting for you to decide to say 'yes' to a meeting: a reproachment an accord and one always got the sense around you Peter that you were carving people up in your head

(but what you could never do was transcend yourself and those judgements and be happy)

so broken by our love by our grief (the love that moved us) I want roses to scatter round me roses to cluster around the day outside: trees bare bushes bare roads sky empty

(mornings inscribe themselves like ink in the flesh)

under the snow the hyacinths are unready and are we still unbloomed like seeds? are we still waiting for the warm May rains the life prepared for to spring forth? no: we are not waiting

watching the snow we listen we move we

mouths crushed the cold on my tongue snowflakes kissed from my eyelids salt warm in my mouth

reduced to a few scattered mental associations Peter

Richard brought it home unwittingly (I think that was in 1985) and of course I was completely horrified and I remember sitting at the kitchen table smoking cigarette after cigarette while I waited for Richard to finish reading it just so I could pretend I hated it (your stupid play)

which was not up to the standard of The Dancer or your poems or the long essay you wrote about Emerson for

and one winter years ago I played Masha in The Three Sisters and said I was dying of life and I put so much into those words because Peter I meant it I really did and Chekhov has meant so much to me I think he was the only man who ever understood me (including you)

but I repeat these things because I'm incapable of repeating anything else (of writing a better refrain)

the language is too poetic: entirely inappropriate for the stage

(what Richard said about your play)

but still that image of you standing tall in my kitchen my mother threatening you with god knows what a pan or a plate or a telephone and you saying calmly that we were just sitting there minding our own business having tea and I remember that was a January day and New York looked absolutely miserable and you said you would walk all the way to Brooklyn you were so mad but I think at some point you must have taken the bus or the subway (that you must have because it was just too cold to walk it really was

and I've had affairs Peter wonderful fucks with older and younger men and men my age and I considered sleeping with a woman once and I have no idea why but I've always liked sex so much (why I've so needed it) but the deeper point Peter is that I have never really been faithful to anyone and there was never anything metaphysical about my affairs (simple gestures things any actress would do onstage) and if you knew if you just knew how faithless I am how faithless I was how faithless I've been (and you do I know) you would never speak to me again and you haven't but I haven't either (spoken to you) and neither of us have spoken to each other for a very very long time and that's a form of faithlessness over and above my own: a faithlessness more like anguish than anything Peter (anguish for what we can't ever bring ourselves to

and the years with you they always always meant too much to

because the weary are divided by the blade of the sky

snowdrops like Roman hyacinths cropping up under the window

my mornings are usually spent listening to Richard eat cereal at the kitchen table so content with himself (so pleased)

and I could have shouted I could have thrown a plate walked out but I never did

on the back of the neck you'd kiss me wake me up run your hand along my thigh stagger the blood fleece the heart

*but to carry myself forward would be to carry myself back
to nothing*

*and we have always been great consumers of flesh Peter
and it was flesh (skin touch kiss) that drew us close (fused
us into one voice one murmur one music)*

*a fire we braided with our hair a fire we passed back and
forth until it was dark outside and remember how we'd
rise in the predawn? how I'd say 'I love you like a last
quartet?' (like the slow part that takes you by the throat)*

*and together we'd watch the snow Peter falling slow and
gentle and it was so good those last winters to be away
from my parents away away from New York and it was
so good to feel alone and safe and I could put my head to
your heart Peter hear nothing else no sound no voice no*

*the moon combed across the floor dragged under a wave
of fire I*

*so I keep repeating that I'm sorry and Peter I'm SORRY
because it WAS my fault wasn't it? marrying someone
else (end of story): but you had this moralistic streak in
you too and that's what drove me away (I was afraid of
your judgements and I still am)*

*and what is a clever book Peter? (a book that receives
you like cut glass)*

inhaling terror with our love our hands were blue (do you remember) in the cold and what did it feel like walking with me through the storm? (blackflowers: hummingbirds of ice:

because of Stanislavski's genius as a director and up to that point Stanislavski had only explored the theme in Chekhov and forgot that in his plays the sound of the rain outside the windows the noise of crickets early morning light through the shutters mist on the lake were indissolubly linked (as previously only in prose) with people's actions and that's all that I wanted out of art Peter do you understand? that's all I'll ever want (that link)

because how we talk (like music) is a sign of our grace

during a performance an actress always draws the audience inside the circle of her enchantment

seal me in your hands crush the daybreak into glass

because when I woke up I was thinking of you

and god I loved that old falling-apart half-heated dormitory house where we'd make love all morning not saying a word the windows all frosted over

like getting drunk on water

and my brokenness is better I think Peter (truly) than my wholeness

and I loved being away from my parents and from the anxiety that was everything the city represented but I came back didn't I (because I never really left)

and how does one even begin to understand how much we lost with each other: how many lies we had to tell to get where we've ended up and do you think it's easy for me now just because I'm divorced?

because great actors are great attemptors just like great writers are because as you told me a long time ago: nothing good emerges from art without risks of the highest order

because it becomes impossibly difficult to say anything true once you've made a move like that the move like I've made and if I could take it back I would but I can't so I won't and

like two vedic birds perched on the limb of a lifetree: merging our voices together for eternity

falling with silent cry into the void-like air this winter morning the moon still perched in the sky

and that seems to be all we get one love then a repetition one thing (then a repetition again) an impression that reveals the magnificence of life that spirals out of us like

*a cathedral tower that we hasten towards not knowing
how far inward we go or how far away from other people
(other lives) we move or how distant (like moons) we
become*

so we'll wake to the stars (cry with our mouths shut)

*and that's it (precisely): the color with which one resilvers
the moon*

*much younger then close to thirty and I was still attractive
and still charming (I aged so well in the beginning) and
I liked having intelligent men close to me (men I could
wrap around my little finger)*

the veins of the lungs reeled out like silk

tenderly pulling off our wintry petals:

*love letters and the smell of oranges the stars split the light
hanging out like entrails*

*a knife which pares away the skin around the eye at
dawn*

*the membrane of morning so close now: nearly beautiful
sorrowfully stripped and utterly white: too delicate like
worn piano ivory:*

*and Love will not let us go unhealed through the world
Peter*

because I want to create inside of myself another deeper more interesting kind of life when I'm onstage

the first was David the philosophy professor who you would've like if you had met him he was just like you except not as committed to romantic unhappiness as you were and I've had affairs ever since without regret

perhaps with men (again) who reminded me of you in not-so-subtle ways and perhaps you've had affairs too that were really entirely about me

and it's a miracle (this emptiness)

and poor David was a wonderful lover he knew just what to do and I'm not sure why I stopped seeing him except because I could

because after awhile leaving people became the only skill I had in love not just a defense mechanism but THE mechanism period

but what I haven't ever done is thought to myself 'this is the result of a COSMIC SCAR' 'this is the result of my mother ruining my nerves for life' no I haven't thought anything like this to myself: I've just believed it: accepted it as a fundamental truth and do you have any idea of what it's like Peter to have THAT be the fundamental fact of one's own life?

*a chord of dissolution: unmystical and uncomplex closed
back up again in a shining wave the structure of our love
the time that has passed around the dark ring of the sky*

*you divided me beautifully into love and death and
you did that to me Peter so that you could really own
someone completely (rather than partially) and that was
incredibly cruel of you but I loved you (my god how much
I loved you) and you never knew (and you knew? you
must have known) but still it feels like you never did*

*then for a few years after we were married Richard
and I lived in the Hudson Valley with other people in
the theater in the community and those years were nice
enough I guess when Julian was a baby and I could take
him for walks and the air was clear and I could ride my
bike to pick up groceries and we could get fresh farm milk
and eggs and no that wasn't so bad it hadn't occurred to
me yet what I'd really accomplished by leaving you*

*in fact it wasn't until we were back fulltime in the city
that I began to consider the possibility that I was haunted*

*the sunlight is so rich and I am happier than a sleeping
dog laying in it*

*and Peter: I do not suffer because life still enchants me
(and do you believe me?)*

because this is simply the merging of words and pictures and the taking of them apart to divine new meanings once they have been put back together

insignificance is everything after one is born

and Love is not like this: Love starts from the inside-out: manifests itself as total indifference

the crush of snow under our feet I still hear the wind beating against the house-slats and the thumping of your heart the fluttering of your eyes the organic motion of your body next to mine: the total process of living and dying together as one organism

and my sister sent me an awful letter just before she died blaming me for so many things and I couldn't believe it because so much time had passed and she was talking about things from when we were children not loving our parents enough not being nicer to her not understanding her

willfully making her jealous with you leaving signs of our lovemaking all over Eliot's apartment even though we hardly ever did it there it was a crazy letter Peter full of bitterness I don't want to sound like that I don't sound like that? do I?

because Chekhov was common ground for us

and it's as if we've fed a microphone through a wormhole in time and made recordings of the sun rising

and the antithesis of everything unlovely: the snow: its choral music wrapping itself up the stem of a skyscraper: the skyscraper then becoming more and more like us

and you were always setting up systems of intellectual mirrors and you used to come off as so unbelievably cold to me and other people

so down to the computer with my morning coffee stockingfeet to say hello to the cat (this is how it begins)

I'll play music we used to listen to and I'll never forget how much you loved music and how much I did too and how closely we associated each note with ourselves and how

the fixed painterly image of myself at 16 17 18 19 I've confused the dates (really I can't even I say I remember specifically when

but of course I do even if I don't of course I want something that

the mind supressing molding shaping containing the sudden and wild dance of The Girl of The Past from right to left on stage and would we begin with drinks with lunch coffee tea a walk? would we simply sit in silence and let the universe fade to a blur?: I don't know you tell me: tell me because I want to know because I'm asking because I've been asking and I'm willing to listen Peter: I'll sit at your feet

you synthesized EVERYTHING internally before you ever uttered a word to me (I wasn't so lucky to get your initial impression of anything)

Richard had an affair in 1994 but I forgave him

when we were still young enough for forgiving to matter for divorce to have meant something slightly more than aging rapidly alone

and maybe it was earlier I forget

blue eyes so clearly receiving my light and the only thing we knew together was TOUCH

that the destruction present in the universe is equal to the creation in it Peter:

and love equivalent to a grain of sand can supersede the whole universe of death within or without and I really believe that I do

but there have always been these fragments of you Peter floating through my blood running perilously close to the heart because it was never easy (it was NECESSARY but never easy) and you have to understand my state of mind when I was with you (I was a very very very needy girl) (and SO unhappy)

and yes I know that I'm not really talking to you but I like to imagine that you can be summoned like a spirit to dance along the walls: palms open in praise of fire

but hurt is something that people don't understand something that I don't understand

and I'll never talk about Clara who joined an ashram to become more spiritual my poor sad sister and I'm going to keep trailing off you'll have to forgive me but the dovetailing it's just impossible to stop so you can try to stop but me but it won't work because I'll just have to keep working like this it's the only way I

you (your poems) were detectors for light (the light in other people)

and something concrete emerged (your touch your written language)

heaving in the darklight your mouth glued to mine I'd cut away these layers of time to go back to IT to you even if I returned to the present emptied of love completely because return trips are always worth it always significantly better than original trips and I like waking up in the winter and I like the cold floor under my bare feet and

*I like watching the steam rise lazily from my mug of tea
and I like writing to you endlessly in my head and I don't
know why but I want to continue and I will and I won't
stop*

*because being a mother means washing your child's feet
and hands and face and wiping the shit from their ass
not sleeping at all sacrificing yourself constantly for their
well-being (their growth): so once you've done that Peter
(been a mother) you can talk to me about sacrifice*

and all of this is too beautiful for me (the life I've lead)

*and did you hear my cry for mercy (black lips buried in
the throat) a sail! sail! did you watch me pass through
youth to now? to a state of*

*it was uselessness (love) and it was sweet how you kissed
me when the sunlight passed through the bedroom and I
think we were always hearing music then: the unmuted
silence of everything the chrysalis of snow the*

*and obviously (you idiot) we cannot impose an eternal
structure on ourselves*

the city foaming outside like a pot brought to boil

*because the eye projects itself through an object and fulfills
it and what does it notice?*

desire then like a sun withdrawing behind a cloud behind the deep sun of the interior life (and so a ripple a birth from within)

Krapp's Last Tape The Seagull too and the Three Sister's later Shakespeare the romances and the comedies (we avoided the tragedies by instinct) these were all the things we had around us during the winters I still remember reading them aloud and I have no idea why we just didn't stay in that mode Peter I have no idea absolutely no idea I wish someone would tell me honestly Peter I wish someone would because if they did I'd be grateful I'd

talking bringing home books from the library studying while I made tea (with honey) and sang to your records and it's unbearable to think about unbearable to think how once one crosses a line in time one cannot even look back over it for fear of

and you were always hovering over me (begging to let you fuck me) and now our old bodies can look through time and not turn away

because the Hanged Man's mysteries are some of the oddest yet most enlightening the Tarot has to offer and they cannot be learned by searching for lessons in the physical world: you must turn within

consciousness is a net dragged along the bottom of a shallow lake

ruin everything for this more-than-loveliness blossom of
yellow Die Blumen drunk in the snow

because we consumed each other we

we rose in the dark getting dressed before the sun was up
the last time we'd see each other forever

during those winter days which felt like last days which
of course they were about to be

time all-warped and ruined by our hope for it

and all I've wanted to know is what you were thinking
about when I walked into the bookstore when I sat down
to listen to you read

(and we couldn't help ourselves from falling like two
stones out of a cloud)

dried amaranth between the pages of a book your book
The Dancer the only book that ever wrote itself for me

and it was a great book (a lot of people really thought so)
and it was the kind of offhand but deeply felt first novel
that people read over and over

containing billions and billions of years of darkmatter
and energy flying around in the darkness freezing slowly
in empty space the heat and motion of animation slowing
to something like a crawl (and it is a crawl from birth
towards death on and on) and I thought I had more

*courage than to think like this Peter but I don't it's not
easy to become young again and reorder this disordered
immanence*

*the winter morning all blueish a golden number all-
forgotten Peter (the children we might have had)*

*and I imagine my email is a knife slit between the ribs
and that it goes straight to the heart and of course I'm just
nervous of course I'd like to imagine that... but Peter I
left you anyway so it's probably you that should go for the
knives and maybe you will and maybe you won't*

*and then brushing away the sinking stars every morning
like ice from a windshield*

*and yes it's useless to be free or comfortable without love
(which for me has always meant YOU)*

*winters holding us physically back from the spring days
that would never come*

*and the spider-veins in my thighs are so red they're
appalling*

*but I can't think like that I can't change what I can't
control*

*the passage of time the aging of the body the last of sexual
desirability*

making a cup of tea reading my email over five or six times spreading it flat again reading it again

wishing honestly that we all could get two chances at life (because two seems like the minimum to do anything right)

the dried fragrance along the kitchen cabinets the jars of loose-leaf tea that I always keep in stock the sensation that I am dissolving into language

because all the years they bunch up and cluster in my head my heart my hands and I want to say something piercing Peter I want to punch a hole in the ice dangle my hand through: draw up a fish

still gasping for oxygen

and I remember you said that you didn't respect writers who could retain total control over their craft at all times: that too much control belied a kind of smallness of soul

with nothing religious whatsoever on the line: and it was the religious that counts in art (the ethical we force inside of the aesthetic) and bizarrely I find that only now do I agree

and I'm just fragments at this point (fragments of your poetry)

*water frozen in the atmosphere pain bearing its cure like
a child and that's what's I need pain for (always pain)
because the unseen world inside of us is willing to suffer
any kind of unhappiness for love*

*and you were always abstract (I saw you from the point
of view of the universe) you were always abstract Peter
because you wanted to be a poet before you wanted to
be a person but I never wanted to be an actress before
I wanted to be a woman I just wanted some physical
humane warmth and was that asking too much?*

*it was Pascal you told me Peter who imagined that he
couldn't stretch his mind out far enough to imagine that
his dread of death could be exceeded*

*mouth crushed the cold on my tongue snowflakes kissed
from my eyelids the salt warm in my mouth your toes
rubbing up against my toes your*

*unconceal your light (your flower) the silence that you
gave to me like a cup of black milk and I'll ruffle the
poem-page forward find the place where I left off it was
last spring when I heard you read it was like nothing else
it was*

*yes dark enough this morning for the dead-in-winter
bird's nests to catch light as if on fire from the sun rising*

*each morning we'd fuck and warmly you'd embrace me
as you came and warmly you'd*

*remember your letters in those days so full of life almost
glowing and just touching your skin then soft as a miracle
(like a mimesis itself of longing) you construct thought
you bind it up in a sheaf of words (then you scatter it)
and*

*snow heavy down around me to bury me and seal me
away and I'd like to be discovered by an archeologist of
mourning*

*but I don't think my mother ever ceased to think of me as
her ungrateful selfish little girl her little girl who*

*and the body before it starts anywhere starts with
awareness and we realize that we are standing inside
ourselves like we're onstage or inside a house or inside a
winter morning or inside the memory of one (a winter
morning a house a stage)*

*just my chance to fashion a spear point out of your bones
(a spear that I can wield at your emanation)*

*puts the burden on our lives to be exciting and interesting
and glamorous and beautifully painful but honestly the
truth is that*

and we'll preserve ourselves in snow Peter as if in salt

(your skin: your blueish irises: miracles of receptivity)

heavily until I resembled Mallarme's flower of absence
my legs over your shoulders my head thrust back your
hands gripping my thighs pulling me closer and closer
knowing that we can't hold ourselves apart that we have
to surrender everything: have to cut ourselves across the
throat pour our blood onto the bed

the snow falling between my fingers your black feathers
purgatorial and maybe for a woman at my age it happens
(a woman needs that kind of reckoning) and soon it will
come to that reckoning among the ashes:

then there's this perspectival flatness that comes from a
cold early morning (which is the opposite of a midsummer
with everything dimensional and alive and overfull with
life)

you needed other woman: I would have left you no
matter what Peter because I couldn't have taken it (I
wanted ALL of YOU)

see the wounded universe staggering above us like a deer
shot out of season

back into you my quiet midmornings my life in the snow
without mercy always coming close to melody it's my
body like an ice sculpture my skin cold to the touch my
face turned away from you suddenly

Richard still wanting to get back together still calling texting emailing but he doesn't know why it's just a reflex a muscle contracting in response to a stimulus

a cutting away of self (or otherness) because I'll bury you in love Peter and I'll recognize when something has died

your paunch your grey hair thickening wrists arm heavier slower less slender less strong the whole form giving way

(the uproar of time in our ears)

it's problematic that I have a child whom I love but to whom the drama of my life (the real drama) is completely independent

the last phase of life: the phase entirely inappropriate for this kind of longing

the winter sky blackening

and you disappeared for years and I sent bundles of your old poems to publishers with notes to publish as received and you've never fully explained what you were doing (why you had to fall off the face of the earth) and can you imagine what that was like for me? raising my son being married to Richard and thinking every day that I would pick up the paper and find out that you died? and I'm not even sure why I thought you were doing something dangerous it was just the not knowing ANYTHING that killed me that made the whole business of separation so much worse and I thought you did it (disappeared) to teach me a lesson and you probably did Peter (you were always one for lessons)

but then The Dancer came out and suddenly you were everywhere again and do you realize how difficult that was for me?

tore me open and you were inhuman and I was

unsalvaged by blood: I felt no disgrace: I felt nothing

wandered out in the blizzard you pushed me down in the snow and we were so cold we could only laugh and we were weightless in time the wind flush in our cheeks our souls strung together like candles in the trees and we touched each other and you said Mariel I love you I love you I love you and Peter I believed you and I still do

because we made an ecstatic bond we fused ourselves at the navel like antipodes

stretched out over the moon your stomach exposed to my mouth

and you were content to let me suck you but sometimes you'd stop me because you didn't like the feeling of greediness that I encouraged in you

the morning shining steadily with undivine light: my husband my house my child: every emotion turned back inward like every day here inevitably does like I'm subtracting something here and that by writing to me... I don't want to be that... I don't want to be lost time... Peter I'm sorry

and when a woman cums she wants to be kissed

and what did all that time mean (the lost time)? the days weeks months years eons eternities lifetimes that wrapped themselves around us?

and I've simply resorted to the techniques of thinking that my instincts suggest to me

I begin to feel caught I don't know if I put up a resistance to this unravelling but it occurs and it's very very painful for me and I can't (I can't)

plunging into absence forever Peter that's what it would mean for us

going back to the days when we received touch and music and light like unopened letters

in you yes loss void doubt: you understand those words are very... (and you've always written clearly...)

so further and further away is all very well but there must be a still point and that's all I ought to have written

through you your lips your skin as white as death and what is the point of constructing these little poems when what you want is ME Peter: can you PLEASE answer that question? can you

so simple when you just think about it (the way we suffered) and I loved you though didn't I? because I have this image of myself waiting outside your house in Brooklyn with mittens on (red mittens) waiting for you to come home and not worrying about anything knowing that you had probably stayed late to talk to your professor (which is EXACTLY what happened) and it made me so happy knowing that I could trust you (which is all I've ever wanted to do)

my consciousness solidified into ice or snow or hail coming down from the morning brilliance and maybe just imagine for a second our mouths pressed together lips wrinkled crumpled up harsh implacable unsmiling and it's not impossible (even close to sixty) to feel like we couldn't try again (that the years would be illuminated in a flash)

a pool of existence: a depth:

running my hand over your forehead whispering darling my darling my darling because Peter I was so so young that first winter together and so romantic and I cared for you so much and my body was so fragile and it was yours it was all yours black translucency like an orchid darkly oil-stained (you)... look in rising fire! look! out unnumbered o' we! reluctant to

no one understands what I've felt: not my son not Richard not you

improvising her music (crazy girl)

only one artist was ever really worth a damn to me and that was and has been and IS Chekhov and I think you were attracted to Rilke above all (it was Rilke wasn't it? for you?) because you liked the way that he made a stunning religion out of people and places and poems and the handwriting on notecards and how he made Art into a High Calling because you didn't believe in anything really did you Peter? so you found Rilke to be great: Rilke that dandy that frivolous boob

and poor Rilke I can't believe you used him like that (just like you used me) and you'll have to understand that I'm bitter yes I'm a little bitter because I find it tragic what we do to people who were deeper better more real than us like Chekhov and Rilke were

the dog to be walked emails to be answered play rehearsal to attend my son to call

and these mornings all whitened the hills the plain with frost and was it a hymn that you sang with your mouth open with your hands in my hands and your tongue in my mouth? (was it a hymn Peter? or just a plain-spoken prayer? (because either way it was miraculous))

(biting me on the neck pulling back my hair bringing me so close that I almost came just looking into your eyes) saving our mercy for the last sin the last possession our last youth (yes loneliness) our last despair our darkness (growing) our wildness (on the verge of collapse)

Richard impressed me because he didn't worry about anything because he was so secure in what he did because he had this very precise (and very flat) idea of what a play could do and this was the antithesis of you Peter who found anxiety in everything and whose art is very round and full and complex

but at the time that appealed to me I'm not sure why maybe because I wanted someone I felt I could master: someone I could control (someone whose silences weren't so fundamentally awful)

and yes that was Richard and he wasn't an unloving father or man but

there are just THINGS you know about a man that makes them conceivable for a particular woman and Richard was just never that conceivable for me except as a tool

:a winter flower my navel arched: my mouth still bowed:

and it's sweet remembering how you sounded in a half-empty room (was it a pomegranate seed? that thrust me into this wintry earth? was it?

mother died before my father last year and soon enough I'll feel more than old and I'll be frail like they were and I too will die (the aging of the body Peter: I can't believe it

our children carry things on for us and I know that's supposed to be consoling Peter and maybe it is for you but at the same time it's like being replaced cell by cell minute by minute it's like being filtered out by the universe grain by grain

working backwards through our secrets our years our seasons

sex contained us and we contained it and we opened it within us and discovered its secrets and I never knew it until I was with Richard and not until his tricks were gone did I really realize

but no you abandoned me first going off to Paris to write your thesis and had affairs with Claires Rosemaries Madeleines (I was so sure) and maybe you didn't Peter (quite possibly you didn't) but you never did anything to reassure me you just went about things as usual and that was your mistake

*and human love Agape not Eros (your god) and I
remember you dressing me in the morning your hands on
my breast your voice in my ear (no one understands how
your poems just scratch the surface) telling me:*

*sewn sapless darkening with soot all forgiven nothing
forgiven nothing forgiven because nothing known and
under the snow I'll be buried when it comes again and
under each word is a voiceless feeling I've known (love
ungentle love) returning bearing grief back unto my body
(love at first so full of light like*

*and there were days alone with Julian when suddenly I
saw things so clearly saw life as it was meant to be and
how my mother took things from me and the way she
ruined me the way she made me so scared of life so scared
of giving so scared of YOU (like that day she caught us
fucking in the shower and you had to sprint out of the
apartment with your pants half-up that was so funny
but it scared me made me feel guilty like I was doing
something wrong like there was something wrong with
a girl experiencing physical love) and my mother was a
devil she was a judge at least she was a judge for me
the judge of everything I did and I can't justify having
accepted (believed) her bullshit for a second of my life but
what can a kid do? and I was just a kid Peter you have
to realize and so were you for that matter*

125

but here I am going through my life still an underconfident girl and GOD how trite that is but how true too

and with David I had this overwhelming feeling of power like 'I'm doing this' 'I'm in control' and I fucked him I really did that poor pathetic man I fucked him until he was bleeding at the ears I left him lifeless (and I liked it I liked having that kind of erotic power)

and like I said: there were others and the feeling was the same (the feeling of power/control/pleasure) to varying degrees and now that that phase of my life has ended I can only look back and

and my memories are of you naked wrapped up in the bedsheets smiling at me inviting me back to bed and I won't

because I have this stupid almost-recurring dream where I disappear into the walls and I become someone else watching you alone watching me

my consciousness of ash and ember and all that was and the gale of the years blowing over us tearing away our skin the muscle the bone leaving us in white light almost nothing (figments of lungs and lips and hands) leaving me to the unknown

but there's a lot of bullshit too Peter that needs to be taken care of little details that simply got lost when we stopped talking but if we ever sit down Peter it will be hours days weeks before we really can begin to understand what happened

knowing that I'm slowing down that my memory is not as good as it used to be that I have to work harder to remember all my lines that sometimes I forget to call Julian back that I've been spending more time in front of the TV or on the computer that I'm letting

and I can imagine what you will think when you read this email:

'pale winter flower' you'll think (something poetic)

no pantomime for loss no constraining of fate

(fire-flecked imagery in the nook of the self)

because it was sex sex sex yes of course it was always your sex your saying 'cunt fuck shit' every dirty word imaginable: fucking me so roughly making me into something incredible pliant incredibly giving

because a woman will give and give and give and I left you the first time so I could stop giving and is that enough of an explanation Peter? that I needed to reserve something for myself? because you used psychology like a weapon you simply cut people in two

and you could do it with a few words especially as you got older and I couldn't face it after awhile I just couldn't

*and you can follow my revisions across the pages here
Peter I'm not covering my tracks I'm not going back and
editing or cutting things out I'm just giving you entire
passages of my inner-life as it is directed and oriented
towards and away from you so that you can read it and*

*and even if that's insincere you can respect my projection
my burnt offerings: my record of flowing/unflowing
speech*

*and around the failure of words we wove music and on
winter days like this I would hear the symphonies you'd
put on while the sun rose*

*sun reddening at the core out of the darkness coldly rising
the land dead the spirit desolate your tongue on my sex
your fingers on my cunt (love just to keep warm before
the radiator kicked on)*

*oh and Julian Julian if only you could meet my son whom
I love so much (who is such a decent caring person really)
and is it so bad that I don't think of him as often as I
think of you? because a son can't really replace that kind
of*

*and Richard was not so bad because there are worse
things than fools (helpless men who cry into shot-glasses
and wonder where the years have gone?) and Peter
sometimes I think that you are one of those worse things*

encoded so deeply in your voice that aorist (your tenseless verb)

reckless birds caught north during winter and what is this impassable presence: this dense curtain like the snow heaving in the air windless? what I am I remembering (nothing) and who are these long black figures swooping? they are the dead (of course): our parents our friends: all like whitened ash because I believe in the light and disorder of the word repeated until quote Meaning unquote leeches out of it and truth remains and all the things we said to each other then begin to quote unquote lose their meaning over time and did we say all that we wanted to say? or was it all a sort of manipulative ploy to get each other in or out of bed back and back again? but getting back to the issue of ploys games manipulations we were full them of course we were we were men and women

and to forgive is not to expect forgiveness but to ask for it PETER because YOU'RE the one who is at fault just as much as the other person is you know: for what you did to them but also you're at fault for BLAMING them for thinking that you DESERVE forgiveness when we are all innocent (if you only look at it from THEIR point of view)

something grotesque maybe just like it was before but our bodies with their petals fallen off their leaves gone their vines withered and so what? if in a thousand different ways I can approach getting old and not just through sex (cheekbones pelvis cunt rectum bellybutton mouth nose ears) because nothing matters in the grand scheme of things because we can't shield ourselves from the radiation blast of time and because we're constantly being overtaken by waves of time and I cannot guess who or what you are anymore

yoga and spin class and spa-treatments and essential oils all of those things because of the stage you know and vanity general vanity

we lacked the brutality Peter (I realize now) to have made a decent life together we just lacked the violence and the hatred that spouses need as a built-in mode of retribution (the mode that becomes necessary in order to keep the structure (the honeycomb) of the family in one piece over time the mode that was so familiar to Richard and I (and you would not BELIEVE the ways I wore him down over the course of

these days like glass (I've turned off the music) and if you write me back Peter please be kind do you remember what I was at fifteen? sixteen? seventeen? twenty-two? I was a mess Peter I was falling apart I was going to a million doctors and had a million fucking problems and all I wanted was for you to love me blindly unconditionally and you almost did that but you had this part of you that *wanted to let me free told me to experience other men and so I did and that was your mistake because freedom was not what I wanted from you*

and I was the girl who used to smile when you moved my hand up her skirt and who'd pull her lip up in bow and take you in her mouth and wipe the semen from her lips and pull you into her with her gasp and

but inside of me there is this terrible anxiety this fear of risking something anything

converting myself into a paragon of absolute and total safety and you won't find that self-analysis is typical of me because Peter I'm always dancing around my own faults and I've got marvelous balance you see

and there were flashes when I went into labor with Julian of you being the father and I still hate myself for that kind of terrible self-betrayal

and the betrayal of you in the first place (the man who was more loyal than I ever gave him credit for)

a blind spot Peter for reasons I can't as of yet comprehend: my words seemingly emit this spurious allure and the last thing I am and/or would ever want to be is alluring or intriguing or even memorable so when writing to you I (unforgivably) dilute and dim myself until I'm almost unwell by it and it was Mahler's 9th (the adagio remember?) when we allowed ourselves to consider

*that two people being together could have some kind
of meaning over and above the pointless sequence that
human lives pass through from birth to death and*

*self utterly broken down clean dissolved and now there's
just this calculating figure who seduces her directors her
audience her friends her family who seduces people and
leaves them*

*and had I grown up in a different house I might've
become the kind of person who buys freshcut flowers
every morning and cries at piano nocturnes and at the
sight of children playing in city parks*

*a man I had an affair with when the towers came down
who lost his wife and you wouldn't believe the things
people say and do when they're grieving it's like nothing
else*

*or like with what happened to Richard: absorbing the
atmosphere of a city gone to ruin (the poor thing)*

*it means almost nothing when projected against the thin
screen outside the snow falling over the macadam the
concrete and over the roofs of the houses and the cars and
over the earth and over the*

*(because that's my own worst tendency and I'd rather
it not be encouraged by others) and what I've been
searching for is an unlovable act of pure self-involvement
incomprehensible (but undeniably artful) an inhuman if*

not anti-human movement that proves that art can exist independent of taste

and so there we are back at lamentations and the hauntings: my mother her white hands folding back the hospital sheets tubes in her arms her airless mouth opening with a gasp trying to glimpse her daughter once before at last THE END

because what we experience is a radical change disguised as a radical pain

my mother's corpse laid before me (I refused I refused to let my resentment out then)

and we'd burrow under the sheets and not sleep at all and we'd talk about dreams we had or dreams we wanted to have dreams of winter gardens trees sagging low to the ground heavy with powder

and what do you think it meant to me to bear a child that was not yours (that bore no trace of your love?)

and have you ever thought that no one is ever like how we want them to be?

and yes you raised me like a father into sexual maturity and this is exactly what a person both does and doesn't want to hear: the paradox that sex is built on (hope and despair: tension and release: you flipping me on my stomach raising my ass into the air biting me on the neck hooking your fingers into my inner thigh pulling yourself into me with a gasp

and this seems to me to be the most tragic way to end a life (dying without love enough to fill one's heart up completely) and now I suppose I'm just waiting for that last languid burst of hope and maybe this little mental fling in the end is just the end of a farce: a signal to Shakespeare to send his Fool across the stage

the snow in Central Park visible from the window my mother making us tea telling us gently to finish our homework (one of those moments where she was sincerely tender with us and we were only little children then and

if only she knew how reckless we were how full of sadness and she did change for a little while didn't she? but then things only got worse when I got engaged to Richard and became free of her control

and that was the worst thing about her: how she would let you think that she was OK when she was really on the verge of falling apart (do you remember that Peter? all the household objects she threw at you all the things she screamed at me?) and that was the reason that nobody including me could ever trust her: because on the inside she was always pledging herself to fate and because she was a good (no: a great) liar and because her will was a will to hurt and be hurt and even back then you were so scared to lose the ability to write poetry because you equated it with life itself and even if poetry and life were different things then well dammit poetry was still your reason for being alive and it was a hero complex and it IS a hero complex that you have Peter but it's driven you to do some wonderful things with your life and I wonder if everyone wouldn't be happier being more like you and if only people could really love each Peter then we could all get through life a little better then we could all be a little more OK and let's steep our love in silence you wrote to me once (and all that shit about poetry redeeming us I never believed it for a single second) (but then again I did)

because a person gets the label 'neurotic' and it sticks for the rest of her life

but I'm not neurotic dammit I'm just a person who has needs and who pursues intimacy blindly like everyone else I mean hell Peter what else is there to say? that we weren't perfect that we fucked things up?

well we did of course we did that's what young people do when they're in love

so I'm sorry I'm sorry I want to cry (but I won't) (of course I won't)

and a winter morning is only a reflection of the deeper instability and chaos of Things (metphysical things Peter like granite dust rivers mountains the spaces within poems silences the meaning of words the condition of the world in our sight the obscurity covering a void (like a pearl dropped in a glass of milk))

and love yes my body is always expanding to your touch and yes I want you to undress me again come close to me again and yes I want to feel your chest expand and contract and expand and yes I want you to stroke my head hair and yes I want to feel your breath warm against the palm of my hand and yes

it's remarkable isn't it Peter how nothing stays in place how no one you ever know stays the same how a kind of anti-stasis is working within us all the time

for it is not enough you told me once to know a single flower: one must memorize an entire field in order to write a poem

then twice like a stone from heaven you came close to me and

the bleakest things are always true in our universe of darkmatter and antimatter: silence resignation fear loss and everything beautiful is subject to annihilation forever

a lie shut like a leaf (the heart dislocated from

catch snow on our tongues lay down unmoving in our silence and life isn't just a movement from birth through to terror: it's a kind of arc that our bodies trace a segment of on their way from

in the dark getting dressed everyday before the sun like it was the last time we'd see each other forever or until the universe burst like tinfoil in the microwave and things started over

because each synapse is its own moment: its own fate

and all we've been trying to do is raise ourselves to the level of Things That Matter and nothing could be more foolish could it Peter? considering it's impossible and not just fruitless but distracting and the bitter paradox is that it takes a whole lifetime to figure this out: that nothing can be anything other than what it is (that your poetry is just one fiction raised above the others (gorgeously) and I could always sense the dancer in me swaying to the music of your touch your words but what does that matter? really Peter what does it

because I imagine you walking through Central Park on a snowy morning your hand on your head to keep your hat (you wear a hat in my version of your life now) from flying off in the wind and you carry a book under one arm and you stop to watch a few children playing in the snow and you smile and no Peter that's not like you at all (not in any way): you are not smiling: you are concentrating very acutely on nothing as with all things: I regress towards the point of another beginning another incarnation of the sacred in the sky: snowform: transparence (imagine it Peter)

you rebelled against me left me in the wilderness of our love and I never understood the shock of mourning before I met you or how life possessed a kind of inexplicable density that I couldn't fathom in you (where the density was limitless)

and Peter I feel like the projector has caught fire and the whole cinema is filled with smoke and I don't renounce anything (I don't) and the more brutal unsymbolic world of emotion is what I live for and don't you live for it too?

and OK Peter there are things I regret about my marriage not just in it but outside of it I regret like not being more honest with Richard not being more kind to him and boxing him in gradually over the years attacking his style as a director his ideas his methods his smallness his unbelievable small-mindedness as an artist because in the beginning of our marriage I was always letting on to Richard that I was the better artist (and I was) and by the time we moved back to New York City I'd broken his confidence (I'll admit that to you) and he used to have all these jazzed-up ideas about sex but I had ridiculed those too (just like I ridiculed his plays) and I shattered him over the invisible image of you that I kept close and private and pristine and Peter don't

I lorded you secretly over other men held you up as an unspoken undisclosed ideal and you like to hear that don't you? and no I don't believe in male gaze theory I believe in nature looking in at itself from different angles

because nothing stands still nothing ever stands still but let's try anyway (to stand still) Peter

and Tom (I think that was his name) sent me flowers after the performance and he met me backstage and it was a truly horrific affair but it lasted for a long time anyway because after thirty I started to get desperate that something in me had started to freeze and the Antigone metaphor yes I suppose it's relevant but I'll have to explain it again later when I'm thinking more clearly and as for this stupid stubborn belief in the concrete reality of a flower a shard of church glass a river a garden well

and then in London for a six week run there was someone else but I won't say his name not because I've forgotten it but because I feel like I'm too short on time to call back these irrelevant names these insignificant choices

and you've always written poems with this crazy doublesearch for innocence and truth in them all at once at the same time and give it up Peter it won't happen you have to admit that you've got to choose one or the other that you can't have both that you just can't because innocence and truth want to destroy one another like two planets yanking at each other's total gravity in space

and I was not entirely beautiful but you couldn't see it
(the little flaws that would deepen with age) and if you
were to really look at me again would you still want me?

or maybe you would because there are still men you know
younger men and yes that IS a point of pride but for how
long at 55 one has to be realistic

and what did you expect me to think with you running
off to Paris to write your thesis? what did you expect me
to do except protect myself? and that was your greatest
mistake Peter: that you thought I would love you despite
the inherent risks (because I wouldn't)

watching you and wanting to watch you because I knew
that you were watching me and because there was this
living thread this something that one could dance up and
down and across as if it were a telegram wire

(small but essential truths that otherwise would remain
undiscovered and since you I have let these truths go
undiscovered (truths that right now I am unable to name
but which I know are

remember when you hit me because I wouldn't stop
crying? because that was the moment when I ceased to
be a child and I've always meant to thank you for that

that first love like Shakespeare dreaming the sky smashed
up snow beginning to fall again and I love the mornings

the spiritual hour I love listening to the snow (the silence)
I love sitting down to write you

you wouldn't believe what I wrote in my journal the
night I came home from your reading and the heaviness
of a stone is the result of its introduction to unity and its
negation of space adheres to a world that is seemingly
empty and nothing seemed more absurd and nothing
seemed more beautiful or unlimited or frail with lightness
than you at your reading like no time had passed like
nothing had changed like we were in bed again together
and you were reading from napkins or notebooks and no
Peter because we were done for good and I'm incapable
utterly incapable of telling anyone what I really feel and
you know that because you're exactly the same way

a surrender to something I didn't understand a swerve
towards something outside of myself a swerve towards
you Peter YOU! and the more time passes the more we'll
need each other and the more we'll need something to
root us back in the present to call us back down to the
ground of the body the root chakra of whatever it is we
are (human or inhuman or both)

and still my slim figure my body like ash reaching towards
you in the dark not touching the white sun at the welter
of dawn because I'll wake next to no one crying (rend the
soft red form of memory with my hands Peter) I'll

and well if you consider the pain and the distance then well why not? (what is there to lose?)

because we return with nothing strangely radiant so we may share nothing are nothing reveal nothing and you always had more and less respect for my intelligence than you should have and how full of mistrust you are over the prospect of meeting for a single measly afternoon Peter and LOVE Peter it chooses us (sweeps through us like a wave): carries us like birds into the clouds

and it was a wound (yes) a flowering a gash in everything we thought we had already determined (and that's the classical image of Eros isn't it? (the arrow-wound))

an aorist swallowed down like some tenseless way of speaking back and forth across time and I can imagine my own death this morning and it seems so incredibly real (like something out of Beckett an old body breaking down into physical tautology the eternal self collapsing into laughter)

why I do relate these things? memory and death? and what else would I have done not knowing you? (even for love you were incomprehensible) and I begin to see them how the dead or the lost (you being lost Peter) stand out and glimmer in the morning light

wanting a theory of pleasure elucidated to me as a theory of life (but who is there who can do that for me?)

under the pillar of this darkness I will set myself down as an urn to receive your ashes

stuck inside the bubble of cast parties and meetings with film directors who need a female character actor who hasn't aged too badly and like all solipsists we were obsessed by our own gorgeous interiority and Peter don't you realize that our fascination with each other came from the fact that only with each other could we get out of our own heads? and not just in a casual way like watching a romantic movie or something but in the sense that we were really truly TRANSPORTED when we were together

our nervous system ran together (through guts spine hands toes) once and my life has formed around you like scar tissue Peter

to kiss you: to draw you inside of me again:

all-stilled in the mind disclosing within myself what I thought was true about us Peter what I thought was absolute fact (but which upon examination turns out to be more and more suspect): that we loved each other that what we had indeed was love and not infatuation or sexual envelopment and there are no absolute answers only suggestions (critical suggestions) and take this one: that whatever we are is still being determined and that our seeing each other last spring was only the beginning for us

at least that's what I gleaned from your latest poems
which my god were something else neither good nor bad
simply

and on the morning of my wedding day I cried while I
was getting into my dress knowing I'd lost you (that I had
done something permanent) and when Julian was born
I felt the same thing but even worse and that was maybe
the worst thing I've ever done (feeling guilt over the birth
of my son)

and are you working on anything now? new poems?
new essays? because each poem of yours is itself the gift of
memory and

how alone we are our flesh naked our bones hollow
because

we cleave from the best images of who we were (loving
and fearless) and at what point do we arrive? at what
destination and here Peter I have a thought for you: it is
inconceivable that ANYONE dies

you used to say that winter was an excuse to stay in doors
and fuck until we couldn't move anymore and that was
incredibly clever of you I always thought (and so obvious)

because it was the great beauty Peter that you said you
were looking for (and did you ever find it?)

my mother her skin yellowing before death my father grasping my head his eyes bright before and another world he said there's another world then (my mother however was faithless)

a path made over a sea of ice no footprints no ripple no shadow

growing cold the sound of the wind a last monotony a last lament this morning sunless like my youth undying and touch me Peter I want to cry:

a memory white like winter so bare and forgotten (that cold landscape strewn with burials)

bodyself compounded into sentences because we were consecrated in each other and my life has been emptied by your absence and what was the last thing my mother said? it wasn't I'm sorry it was so simple: 'I don't want to die' she said

the east-wind straining against the sun this morning so lovely pacing around standing in front of the window not feeling anything not being able even to cry or

being in the midst of THAT terrible experience of recollection all-of-a-sudden out of (no)where and is this a memory deep-down long-leaved (unburied)? like the aura of death (or the snow falling around me unforgotten?)

maybe except for the possibility that

the clamour of the wind and the sound of the neighborhood being ripped to pieces

I liked living on the Hudson in the winter in those first years with Richard: it was so peaceful and I felt the peace of having a son who cooed at me with big eyes who crawled at my feet gripped my ankles cried for me loved me

walking along the train tracks each morning with the stroller Julian bundled up so that only his little nose was visible

not worried about acting or about you or about my parents or even about Richard just happy to be a mother to have given myself up to someone without any conditions whatsoever

and I knew when I saw you again that like Beethoven with his hearing gone we'd thump out our last melodies in defiance: that we'd reconcile those years apart with the ones to come

unprepared for darkness:

the sun rising in the east:

a love of the death within us heavy with age lugging around a body at the point of breaking down into pieces (and longing for it) and did you know that Chekhov was a country doctor and consumptive and supported his entire family and wrote hundreds of stories and some of the greatest plays of all-time and that he never complained without reason and that Tolstoy said that he had the gait of the girl and that Tolstoy loved him (thought him the dearest man he'd ever met)?

a leaf buried in mud and snow this loveliness (gone for so long) bless me: my body of bone and dust

and I can't find the wound you left in me but I know that it's still raw (nerve endings dangling): the wound that you made so that I would not forget who you were the wound you made so that you would know that you would have a place in the world and 'is there not a place for me?' Schubert asked on his deathbed (something you told me once)

and when I did The Seagull for the first time I played Nina and I met Richard and now I'm playing the older woman the woman who is betrayed for the younger more beautiful self that I was and understand (please) that you were Treplev and now you are Trigorin

but Peter Peter there is infinite time ahead of us and back before us

and so often a tangle of wings and voices in the morning: meaning the idea that I could write to you was there but

Richard would come through the room touching me on the back of the neck pausing to watch me write and

I lacked for courage for years and years and years and there was Julian but

enigmatic waves of life passing through me now as if your conscious plentitude of self constituted those waves and you knew what was outside of you and what was a part of you and you knew that what was a part of you was greater than what remained and poetry is a void made in nature and made through us and

I slept with a man I met on the train back from New York one day not long after I'd had Julian and I remember thinking: this is what the rest of my life is going to look and sound and feel like now

a series of affairs and graspings after closeness

not immoral at all I feel: only necessary and only human

according to how we sound to ourselves and how we slip into each other's diction slip into new movements new chords (each shape hidden within the previous shape like the infinities inside a fractal)

and do you think that I've used sex the wrong way Peter? that I've used it to my advantage not for love but for power? because that would be the cruelest thing if you thought that of me even if it's true to myself of course in the

I contacted you once: wrote a letter to your publisher after my mother died begging you to meet me because I felt so alone and I just needed someone who understood what it meant for their parents to be gone and you never responded and I wonder if you ever got the letter?

and there's a quiet stillness living underneath ordinary things that prevents total desolation and you were merciful in a way that I wasn't and I blotted you out as thick as a cloud every transgression and every unredeemed act but now I can't now because you've pushed your way through a cloud of ink you've become a real presence and you've begun to speak to me Peter and not you but the memory of you in me

your poetry written in water turned to ice overnight but it was listening to the last movement of Mahler's 9th when as I remember you broke down one morning and you said you hated me and how much you loved me and that you couldn't be near me anymore (that you couldn't bear it) and though by the afternoon you took it all back but I never forgot it (what you said to me)

slender like an acacia shaking in your arms one bloom left on the tree falling into the water of eternity forever ago I left you in the winter but I remembered you through every season until it was winter again and again and again and yes through a zillion pointless affairs and whatever else bad plays bad films bad moments as a mother that I wish I could have back and Peter Peter Peter where are you right now? because

shaking from this new awareness of how alone I really am

to the point where I even miss Richard (just his steadiness)

a moral death you said it'd be (giving up your Art)

absorbed in your poems like a God at creation and how ridiculous you were then (and must be still I imagine)

and you interpreted the universe as deathless in your poems: a grain of consciousness sprouting in the rough darkness shooting up through us like a winter flower

because you said everything was a voyage like a fire folding in upon itself a great cloud a brightness (a breath) therein: sex touch laughter death birth mundanity of every kind

yet even this unlocking of self into text was

New York City beneath me like a winter garden stripped to the bones of its own oblivion and we are unreconstructed from our disappointment cut off from the core of our love and your words form around an emptiness in space so that they freeze and become snow and how can we (laid across the bridge of time) become hopeful again Peter?

because I just want the fierce closeness of your life all around me

I spread my hands out and I say: here: come and measure the distance between your eyes and mine Peter come (because with it the universe ends our love)

foolish things like what Richard wants for dinner or if Julian did his homework or if I've forgotten my lines since the last night's performance and you wouldn't believe how easily the glamorous and the quotidian mix together

because this is the limit of pain: that life go on without us (unacceptably) that our children go on without us (unremembered) and that the land will not mourn us but swallow us up Peter completely that Richard would like me to move back in but I like living alone and that won't change now and you told me it had an almost crazy perfection (Schubert's Quintet in C) that it was like nothing we could have imagined like nothing a person could understand (how people come of nothingness to be born) and that Schubert understood it all (how an extra cello could alter the gravity of annihilation) and there is something divine in these thoughts and it's like we formed ourselves out of darkness like clay Peter it's like we created ourselves so that we could meet in this life (and is it crazy to think like that (like this)?)

and whether yes or no you don't have to answer

very little being eternal and it's never in the Arts &
Leisure section of the Times is it? it's never what we're
supposed to like supposed to love supposed to shell out
sixty bucks for to see for the third time no: what little
there is that lasts is only visible to the people who NEED
(rather than wish) to find it

your voice your hair webbed around me your voice
singing a psalm for the end of life and I'll never admit
that it was foolish loving you:

you echo in my bones: you mourn in me

and why am I still hurling myself against the air?

(like a swallow diving in the sea)

one cannot enter into such negotiations without risk:

volleying between the was and the will be

and yes so love becomes transcendence becomes our faith
just like our voices in the winter become our hymns

just like the soul itself is like a door to

and my whole body shook after you came and I came
with Schubert on the stereo and you told me that he died
of sadness (Schubert did) which I knew wasn't true but
the emptiness of sex always imposes itself on the heart
and you said words were each of them like icicles ready
to shatter

your hand steadying my sex my nerves spilling out like
angel-hair

and finding these little nodes of interest I

my body still masterless crying with sorrow and Peter I
know that you wrote your poems to keep something alive

*in me and I'm grateful for that (I really am) because all
my happiness has leaked from my life like oil into your
poems which yet are an echo of something better than
me and they give me this feeling of redemptive closeness
and integration with my emotions and do I not deserve
a place on this earth? Schubert asked when he was dying
but I've mentioned this already*

*because we all have these themes that we return to these
themes that we sound like trumpets inside of our skulls
over and over*

*cell walls breaking down hair falling out skin sagging
breasts chin fat hanging down towards the ground and
what a gift mortality is it makes everything so*

*lost the shock of being alive when we lost each other and I
lost the shock of living outside myself and I haven't felt so
alone in a long time writing to you this morning Peter I*

*marvelous how you fell away from me and how I walked
away from you into a new marriage*

*and you'll read my email and then read it again and
print it out and carry it with you on the subway without
really knowing why (because that's just what you do
with things like this) and we need to more than preserve
ourselves in time (I want something beautiful in these
last years) and I will spring from your hands and you*

*may follow me with your eyes until I am out of sight
(beyond the first circle of a normal life)*

*the sky opens with fire and what does this voice inside of
us say? it says: we remain unhealed by time or anything
by violence or loneliness and in the dark we touched and
you were close (the scent of sex) and the fear of losing
you was so strong in me Peter it wasn't an intellectual
thing it was a physical fear and I wanted to make you
a part of myself feel myself protected within your bones
and there are always new loves (new affairs) and new
mistakes and we can always replace ourselves with others
(removing ourselves from who we were) but you (you
know) are always coming back to me (to the gravity at
the center of my consciousness) and I know that in your
thoughts I am always doing the same thing*

*pried your mouth open spit in it and closed it with my
hands and I call it a myth: the myth you planted in me
(your seed running down my thighs) and everything
we sensed touched smelled everything saw everything
decorated with such physical richness (everything that fell
down out from the stars)*

*we were alone together once we let the winter drive us
inside and of all the places we ever were that was the
most intimate by far*

*and as I got a little older yes I became more aloof as I
started to realize that other men were interested in me*

and I forgot a little bit what you meant to me so that by the time I met Richard it was already mostly over I had mostly already grown apart from you and even you (yes you) had grown apart from me and that's the part that neither of us would like to admit that our separation would've happened anyway no matter what because we had begun to take each other for granted

and like a pearl a bead drops suddenly from a string: I drop through the plume of silence into what I was

stars are all exploding as the sun continues rising

and when you cut around my body: be careful not to ruin the thin almost liquid membrane of me

and how mysterious death is to me the grief rips open our insides and this is what I am (nothing) and winter surprises us and the soul again believes in chance not dancing not fate Peter and do you hear it? that single voice within the skull crying out sharply and the whole enigma of objects inside a house or inside a life or a memory or inside a dream lends proof to the idea that there is a metaphysical reality to reality

it was you after all who became like a piece of music and the snow (every grain) is spiraling into infinity (again)

and to touch you would to be to see my life in a flash as if

what you tasted like or the sound of your voice the entire way you embodied a hidden method of living and your voice always had this incredible identity to it even as it changed and remained fluid (like water turning into snow or hail) and I always thought that perception could be cinema like it could be music like it could be anything if it had the right plasticity of awareness but I could never parcel out how I wanted to see you or how to make the connection between ethics and action: action and

instinct for death like a dog heaving on its side birds unsung the harvest unreaped winter scorning all tapering towards the sun

so blot yourself out in the same eclipse that I've watched over and over (the eclipse I wake up to)

because you said that artists needed to get beyond the smallness of being themselves and people slip out of their own happy homes to become like wind and rain and snow and sorrow

and you called yourself a sculptor and you said that consciousness was like marble and what was I to you then?

no pain no resistance no terror Peter no just shunted away into nothingness (no mourning no ritual no ancient rite no burial) not for Antigone not for

carried into this emotion together until it goes dark and starts over

because I move through myself like light passing through a wall of ice diffusing itself into

and we let the harvest spoil: we let the winter come and It surrounds us (Time) and it represents the infinite that language fails to properly denote

and this is what stares back you: fluid as a pool of oil (or life itself): lemon-colored soap and small regrets

because I end up lying

(and how hollow the soul is (like words))

snow tangled in our hair

our nerve endings (bound and lashed together in a circuit)

and for god's sake Peter tell me you aren't still married (I know you are) but tell me that you'd give it up or that you'll let me make you give it up and that you'll remember me the frail girl the girl who would panic and whose heart would race for no reason and whose hands would shake and who

no nonsense words like dirt or semen or spit Peter I won't anymore metaphor after metaphor falling in layers like the snow

those kinds of light and rocks and smells and moods and maybe that would add up to a

because there was so little given to me that I had to take my way to get it

because you've completely interiorized this relation between the human and the divine between the erotic and the seasons that we let pass through us like wind and our happiness was not for nothing was it?

and this pain is like roses waiting in a cafe and I know that you are (that you're waiting for me) and for that matter so am I

in whose sight I made myself known (it was You)

and no springtime in the head no just winter always and at the end of everything when the suburbs have fallen and been dragged with salt will I find your arms reaching towards me in the dark:

and:

I've put Schubert on the stereo again and I don't know why we chose each other ahead of the billions of others but we did and it changed us forever and fixed us into place and Peter can't you see how your poems are lost in the iris of some unimaginable event and how there are patterns in the dark grain of the sky and how I want to return to myself and recreate US for myself (and for YOU too Peter)

and do you remember the last winter we were together when the snow was so heavy when I kissed you on the mouth when you said that I was beautiful with my hair matted down from the shower? because I haven't forgotten how your breath was warm on my cheek and how you held me right there until we were both too cold to say anything else and how I cried 'Peter don't

III. Ben moderato:
Recitative-Fantasia

So let us begin with this, the impossible music of time: the commencement of my voice following yours like one leaf after the other in the wind.

Our two hands pulling themselves together in the sun, unsacred and unforgotten, because Mudflower, the September rains are long over, and this is something else (our being together), and now for my confession: that you were my only creative act.

I wrote to you saying that I forgave you and here you are: a transparent husk, hoping that it is not too late for mutual understanding, the nerves in the small of your shoulders signaling for the muscles to shrink back inside my grasp.

We are always reflecting the abortive attempt of nature to reveal us to us, but never in pure appearances Mariel, always in the creasing and folding back of reality upon itself like a paper swan—

And there you are, at a permanent and yet-still-incredible and wished-for distance: black branches dying overhead, clouds bunched like violets in the sky, and the meanness of hope is in the way we plant it deep within our bodies, never to bloom, or to bloom too late.

And at any given moment, anything in the universe might be called 'love' and at any given moment that object (the object being called after) might be us, Mariel.

So frequently lovely in the fall when you'd come and meet for a walk and my father would talk to you about the literature you were beginning to love, when we'd eat apples with peanut butter and not have a single thought in our heads.

We never called then, we never wrote, and this was a part of Us (the silence of meaning) and now it faces in on us (do you understand?): the miracle of the past, its finality, its difficult existence.

Redlight drawn across your lips like a curtain, and yes, your eyes, I see them too, open expectantly, wondering what they are looking at, what figure, what salient detail, what ghost.

And it's never been worth half a damn to me to be able to use words as beautifully as I could want, because one is always left feeling feckless and scared at the end of it (the outpouring of creative desire) and if I were anyone I would be the kind of person who is happy to work with his hands, the kind of person who lives alone with nature, and who doesn't need people or anyone, including himself, and who is ready to die (to let go) at any moment, like any wise man would be.

Because, you see, we are all falling out of the past into the present, our hands open like parachutes to the sun.

And as you were, metamorphic, evasive, and now for a few more words defined by their movement, a few more words defined by what they will never say: the old chants in the dark, the vanished music, and if there is anyone who stood outside of life long enough to gain some objective distance it was Shakespeare wasn't it? who played the human voice like it was a birdnote chirping from inside a piano.

Dwelling in the dust, rue o' grace: all that I have planted in the ground of Time.

You had your own stories about your father Mariel, but you never were interested in the details of my own, and don't you think that our own children think of us in the same way? as selfish, utterly demanding presences crowding out the rest of their lives? maybe, Mariel, because don't you think that we are the most selfish people we know? never having given anything to anyone that we didn't want to give, never having sacrificed anything (except to each other).

Though we could talk about having punished ourselves with distance, even though we would be exaggerating the difficulty of the choice.

Like a tragedy of unknowing, of never knowing the right thing to do, or say, or the way to even recover one's balance in the process of falling, because we are falling, you have to realize, we're always falling, and not just towards death but towards a permanent disappointment, and this is what Nietzsche meant with his idea of eternal recurrence: that we are certain to all disappoint each other and ourselves forever, and that to endure the idea of the recurrence we need some kind of freedom from morality and a new weapon to employ against the fact of pain (pain conceived as the tool and progenitor of pleasure), and the ability, too, to enjoy all kinds of uncertainty and experimentalism, as a counterweight to the extreme fatalism that we're both prone to (especially me).

And now I know for certain that the soul may die while the symbols of its existence remain: that for every cobweb there is a dead spider.

Fatalism just being a word for the feeling I have that what's lost is lost.

Like an atom cut in two, we rush from each other's arms, carried by shockwaves out of sight: cold tea in a porcelain cup, white carnations, and your wanting more (because you are always wanting more than what experience can give).

No longer living as one composes a poem: with imagination, from left to right, down to the bottom of the emotion.

Weeping in the darkness of the kitchen, hands fluttering over your eyes so as to cover them, asking me, stupidly, to forgive you.

This is what we carry within us: emotions near the source—emotions clear as brookwater.

And I mean that touch is a lost secret and that pain no longer means surrender.

(Because this is what we gather up like broken pottery).

And I'm always wanting to become more humane, less heroic, less willed, and more willing, and I have been systematically oblique with you if only because I never fathomed you out of the depth you existed in, and because I could not accept that you had left me (but this is obvious and it will always be obvious, obvious up until the point of where it ceases to be obvious, where it becomes obscure, and where you question me, and where I break down like a system at the point of its own extreme complexity).

And where were you when I was without any other words Mariel? while your hair was tumbling in my hands? airswept, bewildered into lightness, crying after our seedspeech, caught between motion and use: our chords unvoiced, our throats crying—

Before the music, yes, the music of us—'still gorgeously alive, swept up in the air, compressed within our voices'—

Then, all slowly down, luminous, collapsing.

Not well enough to endure in sorrow, so you came in alone, said I was your only love, tried to hold me, tried to hold me off.

All for the love that we've forgotten, the love that we remember: and it was too long ago to retain much, you realize, a gesture, a sound (a vocable idea caught in the mesh of our near nonexistence), and you kept the flowers (didn't you?) buried in the ground of your silence, with the rest of your unbearable tenderness.

A scene reflected in the retina of an eye: your eye, my eye, it doesn't matter: we play everything backwards to get to the beginning of the tape.

Psychologically I am too secure, too present, too aware of myself for anything to change, and it is THAT (my impossibility) that has kept you away from me, and that will keep me away from you in the future, because evidently I am not really a loving creature, but a shadow crawling up the wall.

Because the texture of the past is like water to you, Mariel (or like the colors you braid together with the absence you conceal), and our eyes can't process these broken shapes anymore, and the birds must talk to themselves, and every ripple of sunlight across the bed is a dream we've never had, and when I begin to tell you about my children, you begin to cry, and you say that you imagine that they are ours (my children), not Daisy's, not my wife's, and I think that you have never seemed more selfish to me, never more out of control, but now, again, there is this voice within that feels almost physical, seizing me, calling me to the external, the full-of-light in you—

Like a butterfly released into a room, hidden from sight, fluttering behind the curtains.

Because our only job (our only duty) in life is to love— 'and please be quiet'—the sound of you crossing the room, turning your back to me, asking me not to leave you like you left me.

Because sex and seduction are different parts of the same thing, like the petals and the stem of a flower.

And this is the mythical space we've built: much larger than the pathetic, embodied ruins of any singular life.

And— 'sick of this stubbornness'— 'so am I'— 'well?'— the cold blue of the ego, and the sky, a way to suggest, yes to suggest: two porcelain teacups (and this is what you lose yourself to: the familiarity of necessary choice), this living dusk, the dust in my eyes, and—'no one jokes around anymore and nobody dances'—because simple arithmetic tells you there are more years behind you than ahead of you, many more, and the body starts breaking down, and you have aches and pains that weren't there before, and little by little the people you love begin to die, and obviously, there are no beautiful surfaces without terrible depths behind them, but even then, it all seems so unfair, so inexplicable, and so poorly planned by nature, all of it, this life, and no, I wasn't like you remember, I wasn't a romantic youth at all, I was pessimistic, calculating, apprehensive: waiting, waiting, waiting for this natural unhappiness to occur.

Our love: like a very bright, prenaturally articulate child.

In one life we have only one sentence and everybody is looking for their own sentence, and this man or this woman doesn't look for a pause, for an artificial, very easily understandable kind of sentence, no, he or she always uses always very, very long, fluent word combinations which are very fragile, but fluent, so that you can't cut it, but then again: our words are tied into knots, sweetness, because of the magnetism of water (the flood of another world)—and—'love me from a distance'—'like piano keys'—'my eyes when you press them down with language'—

Bitterness is not the appropriate word for this phenomenon, I'm realizing now (bitterness being too political, too psychological of a word for what we're experiencing through each other: the pain of the absolute made finite, of the finite made something infinitely human and broken and unrepairable), and it is not a lack of love, but a lack of friendship that makes unhappy marriages.

A sweater and a cotton dress, something I'm remembering now, sitting up on my roof in late October trying to cheer you up (because you were always in a mood in the late afternoon) not knowing that I was gradually becoming too safe and too necessary at the same time for you.

We will never admit (will we?) that we are estranged from our old, unbroken selves, and the essence of Us hasn't changed at all: the essence our world.

Biting my bottom lip when you kiss me: remembering: this is the humiliation one must endure for buried lust, and in all of the greatest works of art there is a supreme expression of suffering and terror that is also, simultaneously, shockingly voluptuous in a way that does not detract from its power or effectiveness: because grief and the sensuality strengthen each other, and may prove to be indivisible and indistinguishable: one from the other.

Shame, I think, is the only thing we will ever share (the aesthetics of unpleasantness).

Something I'm imagining, maybe, separate pasts merging in the solitary memory of your fragile nakedness: and we were strangers until you showed up with your familiar angst about the future, and about me, and about loving, and synthetic consolation (consolation between two people) is not the same as finding it alone, within yourself, as a kind of self-answered prayer, and we believe that we know something about the things themselves when we speak of trees, colors, snow, flowers, and yet we possess nothing but metaphors for these things, metaphors which correspond in no way to the entities themselves.

Because everything that marked our place in the universe will be gone, and these afternoons, which are so painful and insignificant, will again be still, carried on only by the birds.

I cross back and forth between books, or move sentences back and forth between them, and so cause them to permeate one another.

But I've had other affairs in this cottage which I bought with the royalties from The Dancer ostensibly to 'do my writing' and 'have some peace of mind'—because everyone knows that cliches are the glue of marriage, just like they're the glue of adulthood itself, and because everyone knows that a writer needs to have affairs just like everyone else, and that a love of language is a love of experience as much as it is of anything else, and yet, a total, giving love, is the only ethic I have continued to recognize, and the only ethic that I cannot pretend to have upheld.

But you had this image of me as a kind of erotic force when really I was just trying to experience pleasure in my own right.

And that gleam inside of language can go out anytime, like a lightbulb in a neglected room.

Chest expanding, no movement under the eyes, and what changes physically is never our need for air, and the heart, you know, is a strange little organism of interlocking parts.

So I crush you under the weight of my hands: bury you and preserve you in my fate.

And becase Richard will never know (the bareness of the house, the blood marking the door).

Blackbird-black: the soft of your lingerie falling to the floor, your body taught as rope (still): the burying of your nails in my back: the burying of your aging face against my chest.

And we both know that my personal poetry is a failure (because it's about understanding what life feels like, and I don't believe I do anymore).

The luminous outline of the past and how deeply unhappy you are—'what will this mean for us?'—

Bloomless (Mariel) (unaware), my fingers plunging into your sex, your crying for the time that's passed, our lips pressed together, your red sweater on the floor, your dress at your ankles.

Only solitude does not disappoint me, I think, and then, even solitude does.

And given the material character of dying, there is only ever the hope for someone else's arms, lips, eyes at the end: the category of illusion known as companionship.

So you said you needed it: the rose made of paper, the artificial world of marriage with Richard, and it was cruelty as naked as the rain, you explained, what you did and who you chose, and no, not that old bitterness again: just relearning your name, and who you were to me.

It was delivered to us (an answer to 'what is to be done') and we ignored it.

I move the notebook, scraping my leg against the table, asking you not to read what I've written this morning in anticipation of your arrival.

Tracing the surface of emotional fact is useful for me in that it jolts me into thinking, but I still don't think I can ever finish internally the thinking that my poetry begins on the page.

Hungriness that feeds upon itself—'talk to me Peter'—'do you love me?'—that question, like a battlecry.

And your chiding me for my inwardness, my emotions, my Orphic Tongue, my open, Orphic mind.

Breaking free then of every lock, of everything we said we would never say again, or do, and opening all the doors, flinging them wide, wide open, because yes, I'm trying to find a vantage point from which to observe the changing of emotional colors like leaves.

And—'what if we really challenged ourselves to try again?'—at establishing a trust, a bond transcending other commitments?

Family, place, language: these images of who we are without ourselves.

We've perished out of the land, Mariel: dissolved like salt back into the rust-colored earth.

Fear without flight or falling.

Like a revelation, an understanding of something physically embodied in our touch, in your standing before me in the afternoon sunlight, in your walking back and forth across the cottage kitchen asking me what I'm thinking, what I'm doing—'what any of this means'— and what do you expect me to say? because I've never been one to say much, or to say what's on my mind, because there's always this impossible mixture of wonder and terror in everything I'm thinking, there's always this contradictory drive towards despair and transcendence and if I have any Theory of You, Mariel, it's that you're waiting for someone to rescue you from your own inability to choose what's good for you (what's real) and that you're waiting for me, and that I'll never arrive, and that you'll never love me, because I'm always at a distance, always on the horizon, just like you are to me.

Would we want to write Us down to be remembered?

So let me rehearse this: you arrive, I wait for you, you undress, you talk, we make love, we talk, you get ready to leave (ok?): now let's try it again, for real, this time.

The internalized recapitulation of the primative defense that is a casual conversation between almost-strangers— 'you don't have to fake this ridiculous detachment Peter, it does not look good on you'—

Remaining physically responsive to the autumn—'let the light pass through you as if you were a leaf'—glimpsing our beauty, recalling the past, a photograph: tea in my bedroom sandwiches, jokes from an almanac.

We need to explore our conditions and our limits, but we also need this pleasure: the pleasure that is greater than we remembered (or could have ever asked for).

These immaculate surfaces might hold so many polished mirrors up to life but they reflect nothing in particular:

And we could spend days talking about the transformation of the mind into something else: an emotion: violence, exasperation.

If anyone could be close to me, now, it would be you, because I never imagined that adulthood would be like this, that people could bump against the luminous ceiling of adolescence and get stuck there like a balloon against a cloud.

Because every possible stance a critic, a scholar, a teacher can take towards a poem is itself inevitably and necessarily poetic, just like loving another person is, or should be, or wants to be.

And art has come to be a spectator of itself because Art does not know a beyond:

So trace my nerves out in red chalk on the floor, ask Eros down from heaven: give him a new name, a new appearance.

And you aren't only what vanishes, you are and you aren't something that has its own internal, spiritual structure, and we can remain like this, but not for too long, linked together at the navel, bellflowers in our teeth.

You plead for me to touch you just beyond the curve of the visible and this is a vow as clean as sunlight: this begging to be responded to with care, and all that is accessible in you is as pure and imageless as a word uttered at Creation.

Then, when you officially left me for Richard, I started writing The Dancer because I was desperate to retain contact with that essential thing, not just you, but our corresponding youth, our lightness, our lunatic wonder, and a person only gets one book like that, really, one can only write the same book over and over, the same book of supreme disenchantment, the same disavowal of a universe that cannot stand to be exactly what it is, even for a moment: the same universe that is always producing masks for itself, producing planets and people to distract itself from its ever-expanding emptiness, Mariel: the universe we inhabit.

And it could be, but it won't, and I'm thinking of the way my son chastised me once, when he was a teeanger, for looking at a young women across the pool at the hotel where we were staying on vacation, and how right he was, essentially, that I was an embarrassment to his mother.

It's bumping up against the fact that you die alone, and it continues to refute all the little efforts you make in your life to be happy and have friends and pass the time.

And I've always been able to retain a little bit more control and coherence in my life and work than you, but you have to know that it was all only ever a trick.

And yet I could still pull the soul from you like silk: watch it float over the bed.

Your wings flawed with sunlight, your fingers smeared with blood, and your smile: so reckless.

A wild, golden script: a cognitive disassociation with the Beautiful, and what a dumb thing (crying there with your legs open, so creaturely, and so inhuman).

So break a dark glass over the crown of the skull: our life will still be maimed by hunger and gnosis.

And literature has disappointed me, New York has disappointed me, and teaching, and friendship, and marriage—'everything Mariel'—and I genuinely want to know if you understand the consequences of this fact as it relates to you.

'I almost turned my car around on the way here'— 'Maybe you should have'—'Maybe'—

Touch that is not quite sexual, and yet full of impregnable meaning.

Not so white as an anemone petal, your body, Queen-Anne's lace, or just like it, and it's not question of It, because there's no blemish still, on your body, no stretchmarks even, but still: you are afraid (of my seeing), you are afraid of knowing that your beauty is gone, and I don't blame you.

Nature's principle of power: the sublimation which achieves its homeostasis in the transposition of our metaphors for Time.

Because—'once Julian got older'—loving Richard became almost irrelevant, something less than a duty and—'closer to the habitual narcissism of believing yourself to be superior to your spouse'—

Heaviness is a screen we throw around lightness: a virulent form of romantic kitsch.

And all I can do is use my memory to fend off the sinister, underhanded process of decay: the triumphal progress of the wrecking process, the power that ruins houses, walls, trees and fields, and tell me if I make sense (if you can feel it too) and if today is really about preservation, or if it is about something else (disintegration, annihilation) or a third thing, something I haven't thought of, something I cannot even begin to understand.

Not an abstract set up of relationships, no, an activity (loving) that is ongoing and never-ending or shouldn't be that should go on forever even after we die like a bacterial colony that splits and splits and splits until it grows over the surface of the earth and works its way deeper into the workings of every other living thing.

Pick the coltsfoot growing under the train tracks, peel the naked skin of of a strawberry: this landscape is something you must seek into before it reveals what it is—

Dreamless heaps of pictures, cutting you into scraps, rearranging you on the wall and—'what is your next book going to be about?'—'there isn't going to be another book'—'why?'—'I don't know'—

Because desire, at least psychologically, has an open-endedness to it, an unclosed-ness that we have never properly recognized.

I am not clinical enough to avoid love, to pare sex away from love like skin from an apple: I am too heavy, too much like the wound, and too little like the scalpel.

But then I hear music and I think that every nihilistic thought has been a double negation and that a real, charitable goodness has always been before me, open, waiting to be read and read into: it's the discovery that when the leaves are dead the uncreated returns, and by the time winter arrives I'm not sure I'll ever have another (a third) hope of seeing you again, because instinctively, this (today) feels like an emotion that can only be experienced once before it disintegrates, so, yes, these, my thoughts, are a lament (in the sense of an attempt to contain a person after they're no longer reachable).

Each of us constructs a physical world out of a spiritual immanence, unpeoples it: lets it float back into the sun.

A persona that somehow avoids being vulnerable to himself even as he contemplates vulnerability.

Utterly emptied out, a hollow vessel: the language we're speaking—'and obviously, without rationalizing it too much'—we are tied together like two lead balloons sinking into the loam of the earth and if not for each other we'd be alone or worse, except for our children, who are nearly grown, and will soon enough have families of their own to worry about and it becomes necessary for you to place a hand over your mouth to keep yourself from saying what you've resisted really admitting for so long, that we are following an iridescent thread along a path of days, winding down, slowly but inextricably towards the mouth of the underworld, towards that beautiful, blueish light.

But I'm not going to say anything more, or maybe I will, because talking is always an unfolding process, and a process of lying and revision too: like a protein calibrating itself to the needs of a particular part of the body.

A man gives himself to the strength of sex so that he may whisper the names of doves and other household birds.

This process is more haphazard and laborious, no longer spontaneous like before (of course): an act of art rather than impulsive desire.

Inscrutable, like a grandmother's singing, inscrutable like the river, like the Hudson sweeping underneath us, sweeping us on, my cottage, my stacks of books: this place where I go to be alone: where I go to have affairs, and this is the loving strangeness of being together, detached, surrounded—'I haven't been in love with my husband for years'—'Can you make a drink please, Peter?'—while you're studying the photographs you brought (and why?): studying them so that we can avoid saying anything more: why you've come, what your husband thinks, what my wife thinks (all while we're looking out on the backyard unmade like a bed).

The innerhusk of the sun is red, the reddest, like the red of the late autumn leaves.

And would I live this life again with both of us still in it?

Then you're telling me about visiting your old auntie recently whose legs have swelled with water (to the point where they are actually leaking into her shoes), and we are both afraid of saying it, but I can't help thinking of it, and I assume that neither can you: not that time has accumulated, but that it has reached its culmination.

Because what you refuse is everything I accept: bird, beast, flower—the last afternoon light breaking open over the lawn, the summer left behind like a lost dog, and I would like to savor the shape of your body, the not-unpleasant closeness of your navel bending under the force of my hand, but the stops and the chords are too soft, too evasive to leave a final impression: and when you leave this evening I will be left still tasting, still relishing, still hearing, and I'll be left hanging in the middle of the exposed, improvised structure, left singing to you despite the absence of a real voice, left speaking to you Mariel, despite the absence of anyone to listen to me.

You, me, our parents, our children, our spouses: all floating up before the eye of a universe which has no arms, no hands to grasp us with except those of Death itself—'and in that case, Peter, I'll miss the thing by waiting for it'—

And I'll remember this as the the fall when the light was strong and the trees were dying saying that—'You can write honestly now for first time in your life'—

And the leverage you have is that—'I need you to create the kind of life I admire'—

The inner-stress is like a watermark: something that distinguishes us, and do you ever think about the generations, the many, many generations that grew and up died exactly like we have?—'without knowing a thing about how to live, and yet with a parochial understanding of time and place?'—with the narcissism that is inherent and natural to people who remain locked inside of themselves their entire lives, unwilling and unable to get out, to go beyond themselves, in order to THINK for a second about where they are.

Your hair unbound then, falling through my arms like rain.

Unmoving like a deer, darkly, poised there, beholding the poetry of the earth, the reddening of your body inside consciousness (awake)—halfgesture, halfmeaning: the substance of color, the lyric of emergence and the land stands still, the autumn sky breaking open—'Look how the sun follows us from room to room'—wrinkling your face, trying to discern what I'm feeling, trying to discern if I'm feeling anything at all, and it's fair, I think, Mariel, to ask yourself that question—'just like it's fair of all of us to ask that question of ourselves'—because real feeling (true emotion) is almost indistinguishable from the measure of choral mass, from a curve in a baroque structure: an organ, a throat, a violin: blueiris blueteapot, steamhissing, your mouth opening: yellow apples cut in strips, placed on paperplates, and —'What are you thinking?' —'I'm not thinking anything Peter'—

So bring the last orchids, bring the last foxgloves of October, bring all the last flowers: lay them under the cedars, wish them into dust, and let them speak to this: our lust, our isolation: the sun in the trees (the sun in your hands), and—'why are you here?'— 'Because I am'—and—'I don't blame you for hating me'—(words covering every available surface).

The last movie we ever saw together was Days of Heaven, as I remember—'but we had stopped going to see many movies together by then'—

I'll dismember the last flowers for you so that you may knead them back into your flesh and be lovely again.

And no, I could never write comedy, never in a million years, not even in the false sort of Chekhovian way of writing comedy, which is to not-so-covertly write a tragedy on the sly, and then to deny that one has done it (written a tragedy) and this closeness falls further from love and all that has been wished away, or wished for too single-mindedly and heavens, Mariel, your whispers have come from across the lawn all throughout the afternoon, flimsy like newborn butterflies.

I have eaten salt for days, but am not yet full.

Only, you know, like a stone Buddha, your hands folded on your lap, telling me something about release, and so I've stripped myself of every condition but this: that you remain here with me today and somehow, except for the duration of the adagio, we'll keep dancing: summer night, winter night, it won't matter much to us.

The country folks a-courtin' and sweetly you move through me speaking to, caressing me, like at the last judgement, and local apple boughs with apple (and the countryside is finished, as they say).

And under my touch, remain as naked as the autumn itself, shedding its leaves, and when all else fails we'll still have thirty years of smalltalk to catch up on: thirty years of wonderfully pointless chatter about how we've constructed marvelously sturdy lives, and you would adore it if I accused you of lying or betraying yourself right now, and maybe I will, and maybe you really will adore me for it, and maybe you won't, and maybe I'll disappoint you totally, because there are so many moves available to us right now Mariel, that each of us remains frozen, perched above the board, unsure of where to go next, worried that every move, no matter how available, is a false one.

Unpurged: the different colored leaves, like coral, falling (because the universe is hugely alive).

Wild innocence: the wickedness of coming undone (because desire is fun while it's not ending).

And that's what the infliction of pain is: the unmaking of the act of creation itself.

Tie a poem like a balloon to your ankle, tether yourself to the sinking earth, because what was once surrender is now an emotional release (uncanny: near oblivion) and really to talk like this is unbearable once one begins to overhear oneself (Dalloway flowers and everything else, you know: eyes like a crucifix) and Mariel, tell me, are you going anywhere that is truly new to you?

Then there is this emergent quality that is as careless as our love is careful, this inner-quality that doesn't recognize itself as what is, as the willful determination not to be determined by fate, and what do you think my life is like as a married man Mariel? it's sex three times a year, a dependence on pornography, a constant need to justify my instinctual desire to look outside the marriage (and I honestly wonder if it's any different for Richard).

Because I had this vision of being free that I haven't upheld and I would have liked to have been indifferent to everything but my art.

Yes we were coming through to the other side, emerging into that reality we made up in our heads, that we sealed in a bottle with our bare hands.

The self will be erased, dissolved, undone like a knot into a single, silent string.

Placating you with Glenn Gould on the sound-system: the windows open, warm air traveling back out into the daylight:

There is an inherent quietness in you that teaches me how to speak.

Your face turning white like the sky drained of evening.

Willfully, each of us misunderstood, each of us misunderstanding.

A last attempt at rediscovery: eyes, hands, genitals, cunt, nose, lips, cock: sunflowers shedding their last yellows, talking about your son reading The Dancer, and being reminded of you (his mother) without understanding why or how that came to be the case and—'there's too much daylight between us, too much practicality and expectation'—'so go back alone'—and an old man becomes who he always was: sower and reaper of days into hours, hours into buds of blown flowers, buds into waves of loveless and dreamless sleep, and again, your voice delicately, arising—'Peter I was unaware…' — right before the consummation comes: your body under my eyes, your fate under the guise of my strength—'Yes, writing is a form of therapy'—'Well it's not working very well'—

Figura: a sign referring in time, manifest and present in its own context, just as you are: pulling your stockings back on, combing your hair behind your ear with your hand.

I would be happier as a sick, weak man—'like a saint in Dostoyevski'—than what I am: taciturn, overly self-aware, awake in the dream of a successful existence.

Write a character for yourself, that's what I've done— 'what we all do'—and edit it until there's nothing left (amor fati).

You're like a mechanism of insight—

And if we find ourselves weeping? well that is just the miraculous state of being alive, the only proper response to an autumn day like today, very close to perfection, and each of us will find a different kosmos through the eyes of another, and there are very old gods, Mariel, in the rustling of the trees, and the smell of the grass, and living in the walls of this old house, and the sun is very near at hand (even behind the clouds) and I'd like to watch you spill out of yourself again, into the fields, sink half-deep in the cyclamen.

I want to shout that there's nothing I've ever loved in this world except you.

So windthrottled and blueish the sky, still trying to flood itself with a more absolute blue-without-clouds.

But I've never been able to pin my thoughts to the wall and draw lines of analysis all over them: there is no map, no topography, no history—'not even my books'—for what I've experienced and failed to experience through you, and it's my own damned fault that I'm a late late late romantic who has failed to live up to his own utterances on beauty, truth, and power, but even admitting that, I can't help but look for someone else to blame.

Because there's a border, and beyond this border the beauty is almost unbearable:

An obscure continent hovering at the horizon of the water, the ship never arriving.

And what if I had died in a car crash at 25? nothing would be different, except for you (because my books will mean nothing after I am dead).

Yet, not to annihilate myself utterly, because it is not humbleness inside of me but the burden of bringing a thing to nothing as from nothing, and maybe the Good have let the Bad win, and the world has gone to pieces, and maybe people just die with the thud of absolute finality, but then again, then again, we are here and we are alive, and we have this almost unheard of strength to love again, and if that is not SOMETHING, then what is?

It is difficult to determine at what point the manifold awareness of our existential heritage, the heritage that we otherwise call 'our history', will become totally submerged in an atemporal present, but it seems fair to say, very approximately, that our sense of ourselves as historical creatures, creatures with our roots in a deeply uncontemporary (that is to say, deeply untechnological) past, is receding from us every day, Mariel, further and further, like a pond drying up in a draught.

Because, of course, there's this revelatory fear of having never loved at all, and the fear is so deep, so essentially part of the human-composite being, that one has, just HAS to reject it implicitly out of the growing awareness that to accept it would be to admit that one's life has simply been a waste.

And probably, without music, life would be a mistake, like the scent of lavender growing around the house, or the scent of your hair, falling over my chest.

So austere in the afternoon sunlight, standing naked in the living room, because we never called, we never wrote, and you're always scattered Mariel—'that's true'—and outwardly, I'm serene, but privately, each of us is equally desperate and equally out of control, not knowing how to make manifest the intelligent tenderness that would be our only consolation now, and it is impossible to suffer without making someone pay for it, because every complaint already contains our revenge.

The enchantment of water and air, the enchantment entrenched in real emptiness (subtle and unpreceded by any quartet of creative hands).

And so slip into the fields, open your hands to this desire, let the wheat buds cut roughly against your palms, open yourself to the sun shining like an unraveled knot of light—'I feel the shadow of your consciousness Peter'—

The spectre of self in one's own writing: the spectre of death itself.

Rilke, remember, Rilke awaited his poems like you awaited your lines, like you awaited an orgasm, like you awaited my voice in your ear, my hand on your ass, on the small of your back, on your neck, riding you down into the softness of the bed.

Poetry being a discourse on mourning Mariel, and it was on Saturdays, if you remember, that we would go to the public library and read all day, not feeling it particularly necessary to exchange more than a few words to each other (words at that point being redundant).

As a teenager I collected pornography from magazines and mixed those photographs with what I cut from books of poetry, and this is just proof that you should never see me as someone who represents humanism—'any humanism'—in any absolute sense, because, no: I was just a more intellectualized representation of the all-consuming hunger that America itself, in turn, is (and will continue to be) the representation of:

America being exactly what you and I are: manifest greed.

And I'm waiting for that moment of awakening, that happening-upon-an-idea, that is indistinguishable from literature itself.

My father wrote, yes, but he gave me no real formal introduction to literature, because I was supposed to know it automatically by being his son, I guess, and I did somehow blunder into it when I was about six or seven years old without asking first, without knowing why, by starting a journal, and it was a beautiful journal, so beautiful that I didn't want to sully it by continuing past the first page, and I tried to write an introduction to a new edition of one of my father's books last year, but I felt like I was betraying him, so I stopped and let someone else do it, and they did.

You know I always hated the Romans and loved the Greeks, but we are just Romans masquerading as Greeks: we never had that lightness or skill in improvisation, especially with language.

And yet knowing you has made me live in a larger, a more fantastic kind of world: one almost uncanny.

And—'nothing is clear, no'—everything's so goddamn confused, contingent, inexpressible, and our language, internal or external or written down, can't get at what we're experiencing without arresting the fluid mobility of those feelings, because a man turns into a writer by editing his own texts.

But that's where art comes from: life stories.

The major roads blotted out by the occasional car, an old woman on a bicycle, a stray cat slinking around the corner of an old, old house, and once one gets to talking it's impossible really, to ever stop, given how much of the unsaid must be said, and how much of it has been waiting to be said.

Complex fictions resemble complex truths (perhaps they are even the same), and—'it's like we're conspiring against our own memories'—poisoning the wells, setting fire to the town centers.

Because the plasm of life and death intertwine in you, and—'losing one's hearing means first of all, losing music'—(like losing love) and the—'sheer sweeping loveliness of all that the music entails'—and we are as pure as that: as pure as what we believe is possible within.

And what is the interconnection between number and space? between now and then, between sensation and idea? there is none at all: ours is a discrete and determinately lonely universe.

But don't think that it's pain that I'm thinking about, because pain is too banal for this grieving-within.

A quality like a spiral: a shape that emerges through a queer kind of mathematical order (eyes like zones of sunlight: a devotion, an understanding).

I tried to write novels, or stories, even as a small child, there may also have been illustrations and a puppet made out of dead pheasants' wings.

Sunshine bands and stripes crosswise over the lawn, blown back, falling again: that voice, merging with the dust so as not to blind and confuse, and here is the dualistic disintegration of things into a surface: a profound meaning hidden somewhere deep inside of the things that never existed.

The aphorism is a brainwave at a crest, passing the threshold of paradox.

You are your own, unified poetry Mariel.

Throw your dust across me (my body laying in the yard), and—'brood, my Lazarus, on what has come before'—

There is nothing I can tell you about my children—'my son, my daughter'—because they will never know you, because they can't know you, because your relation to me, at least to them, is wholly unknowable, because it is related to a part of me that died before they were born, that had to die, anyway, before they were born, so that I could give myself to them and not to you (never to you).

I read a lot of Russian literature and quite a lot of German too, also writers like Nietzsche and Henrik Ibsen, when I started seeing you, that first year, and I remember D. H. Lawrence being a phase too, and Beckett later, and Borges.

The smell of the rain along the highway on one of our roadtrips is coming back to me now mixed with rotting leaves and I remember you in the passenger seat smoking a cigarette, and you are always returning (aren't you?) to me: like a child disappearing down a hidden garden path.

And I know that you have this tendency to place yourself squarely in the present of your past in order re-experience everything exactly as it was, but for me, distance always intervenes too strongly, asserts itself in a way that negates my strength, and like two brute animals, we are both closer and further from the human heart than we realize (from the pain of wanting nothing else on this earth but what is already ours).

Now, I am like one of those birds that had once been men: their language turned into songs of beautiful nonsense.

The weather, people, objects, natural phenomena, and much that might seem mundane beyond mention, informs everything in my books.

Like what Mallarmé talks about: using words to create a surface that leaves an impression in the mind no matter what the words mean.

Unborn: the old self still haunting me like crazy: the self that was never given a chance to merge with the nature inside of it, and around it, and before that deep, first cleft comes the invisible wound that really kills you: prior to pain, prior to any real moral fatigue, because life lives inside a mood, and this is the C minor of life-itself—'this stupid, stupid playing at being-in-love'—'this wonderful, ecstatic emptiness'—

Perspective means that our attention, when it is intent on something, becomes fatigued much sooner, wandering off somewhere far away, somewhere into the Earth or onto the Moon, this voice, my voice, your voice, exploring unexplored territory, charting regions of passing unhappiness, or passing happiness, or whatever it is, unhappiness inside of happiness, a happiness supplied from without, or within, an uncurrent of physical pleasure like a lightbulb under a lake, and this bitterness eludes you: takes you by the throat.

It was on the Metro North yesterday that I realized that what I was hoping for was this 'and-there-she-is' feeling that I'm experiencing now with you: the semi-transparent past burning through the veil of the present, illuminating the betrayal of my wife and my children in a way that makes it seem less significant than it really is.

The ethical and the aesthetic being two pins which I've perpetually pressed against my palms not to draw blood, but to puncture the salient regret of losing you, and I'm not Peter to you anymore, but simply the nameless Other, pressing you close to himself, trying to recover himself in the overwhelming wholeness of your unnurturing physicality.

Grain by grain, leaking into the ground, like water from a broken cup, the mouth slit through with a thread of fire, the summer sleeping in the trees, the light growing colder everywhere as evening comes on, and if a person takes from the whole a pebble, the leaf of a tree, a discarded cell-phone, it becomes a micro-transmitter which suddenly is broadcasting an unexpected program, broadcasting the world that we know, as well as that which we do not know (that which lies behind cognition) because we abandon, neglect the eloquent surface of things (the flood in your hair, the vinegar in your mouth, the lament on my tongue).

The past remembers itself as we remember it, and we are the past projected forward: the past as a projection of itself: a delicate, synthetic form of past and future: an adhesion of unstable, unpredictable substances.

Especially for you, there seems to be the dangerous possibility that, having made a decision, having chosen to act and now having to live with it, you'll end up holding onto this choice—'this one attempt at happiness'—with too much fidelity and faithfulness, all because you chose it.

And a literary gift?—'no one important or close to me has ever really given a damn about my work'—only caring, really, for their own, personal association with— 'what-I-represent'—and not the nature that I still hope to represent to you like a too-honest dream.

But even if I waste—'literally throw away'—days, or weeks, or months, or even years, I am steadfastly, unconscionably, stubbornly, dedicated to the search for happiness, which I've learned to hold higher than the details, than the surfaces and the moments of our lives in which happiness appears.

Because once you cut my hair: made me sit still in a deck chair, laughed at me, told me to hold still.

But I already knew that something had begun to unsettle, that you were interested in going beyond me as a way of going beyond yourself, and that was what you did, what I knew you would do even though I did nothing about it, because I would not give in, because I would not admit that I could not stand to be alone, and I can't remember the last time I bought a book of poetry except to fill in some requisite gap in my theoretical understanding of the subject.

And the difference in the way we talk, think, move, relate-in-general, now, is astounding (just as the similiarity is).

And internally, I have always pitted solitude against loneliness, always hoping that solitude will win.

Unstring your lungs, weave them up the side of a mountain or tree: the danger of breathing with the earth is seeing as it sees, feeling as it feels.

And with us each new idea fulfills a need raised by the last, while leaving others still open: a continuous game of symmetry and asymmetry, expectation and fulfillment, hidden beneath the innocent surface of touch.

A spline (I read recently) is a mathematical term for a smooth curve in space, but it's sort of time-based, a three-dimensional algorithm just like a poem is.

'I disclose my light to you, my astonishment at your images'—'and you know how much I loved you'— the woods today are sweet with violets, and—'You've always shared the American genius for incorporating everything you love into your writing Peter'—and we're down to the last stories, the last excuses, the last avoidances, and soon enough we'll be left with only each other, left with

the lucid shame of weeping over the things that WE let happen.

A Buddha at rest, telling the moon to cease its dancing, Mariel: a Buddha telling the autumn that all this is YOURS, your consciousness, your sublime existence, because the desire to wound oneself can be interpreted as a desire for ACTION instead of a real wounding, and yes, we are dumb to the man about the possible range of tones predicted by the body, but this is our second attempt at compassion, and I think we might pull it off (honest-to-God), and when my father died I thought of writing to you, but my daughter was starting high school then, and it seemed too unkind to her and to my whole family, really.

I want to ask: how could anyone, anywhere, ever be sick of thinking about love, when love is the surest and truest, the most intimate, path to HAPPINESS that we have? How could you, Mariel, the one who implicitly, perhaps even wordlessly, taught me to seek HAPPINESS, be tired of thinking, of talking, about love?

And this is the ecstasy of unreason, the dance of the soul around the circle of the body (the wind, the murmur of autumn), and the process is so malleable that you can produce anything from anything: love death surrender joy, and note the light behind the trees, and note how we might free ourselves from the physical constraints of absence by sitting at the edge of the bed and not speaking with—'a kind of authenticity that is slightly inimical to that period of our lives'—

Each time we copy ourselves, we make an error, and the mutation persists—'melon-flowers and pumpkins in the side-garden'—and so careless, isn't it? (the glory of nature), and we are withering among the leaves, and people (anymore) don't have the seasons to cling to (the wheeling of the sun through the sky), and we are winding, winding through this long procession of falling leaves, and now a salad with farmer's cheese and radishes and olive oil, and—'Were you really that surprised?'—and—'Did you ever think this would happen?'—and this is what we retain: the warmth of the early fall, the music of our last beginning: the end of something we refuse to understand.

And we are always thinking of the dead who line the skin of the earth:

And how unpetal'd, how tenderly, you—

The metamorphosis of soul into myth is quick: being compelled by some innate music.

An anti-pathos: the body sealed by touch: as muddled and bleak as it is consolingly accurate and astonishingly beautiful.

A stepping stone, a cup of tea, a hand through your hair, thirst and hunger, speaking straight to the point of our understanding—'No one writes like you Peter'—'No one who writes has felt isolation'—

And in quite a naive way I thought I was making a model of Time when I wrote about you.

Clambering onto my father's lap, smelling his colon—'I was maybe six or seven'—thinking: 'this is happiness' and 'things will always be like this' and knowing, somehow, that I would never be able to think those things again, and why am I telling you this now?

Because I never told him that: that those were the happiest moments of my life.

And I imagine that in the minutes before death all the shame of a person's life falls away like a curtain.

And you are gorgeously, disturbingly complex, Mariel: you are like the spiral in a tree, a pattern moving towards an abyss, and I feel very very remote from my own actions with you, as if the shock of being within an enclosed space with you again has forced me to recoil inwardly even more than before (more than ever).

And because we are hurrying on, stripping each other of secrets, stripping each other of the right to be totally alone within ourselves—'Will you tell Daisy?'—'Will you tell Richard?'—

And surely in a flood of great water we will find each other again in Time.

This is your prismatic way of looking at me: your lying, your childishness, your standoffishness, your sex: a heart detached from its veins like a quince blossom from the quince.

The branches of the Sycamores like the arms of a dying girl waving overhead:

This language of hope being at the same time the language of home: the mind always mapping the ground it walks over, the ground I walk over (X), the unspoken ground the ground I won't name (Home)(the past) (You).

Distances between stars: distances between leaves—'I heard The Seagull was a huge success again last winter, so congratulations'—'It's so good to see you'—'Crush the leaves so that I can taste their death'—take the autumn flowers, dry them in the sun, speak with uncommon sweetness—'love has spoken our silence away'—delicate as breath itself: language from far away: all gathering, all consummation: because it falls from heaven (love): the elms after the blight, my father dying, the leaves dying, curling into knots, Daisy with her morning sickness, my son with his tonsils out—'Paint your body with violence'—'Shower me with leaves'—'Sweep me (finally) into the gutters'—

I shake down the mellow fruit tree: catch the pits of the fruit already-eaten on the vine.

The dark assimilation of sensory memory, of your physical weakness, your emotional frailty, your psychological weakness, Mariel, during the fights we had, which, even at that age, came so close to violence, fights which were, in themselves, manifestations of an unhappiness that moved in us like speaking gods, an unhappiness that was as natural to us as anything, and that we still retain, and that is here today, underneath the surface of our skin like veins.

The rushing onwards of memory, voices from nowhere, sensations embedded in the skin:

Every afternoon, that I'm alone here in the country, or what's left of it, you know, in the small spaces left between the suburbs, I'm struck by the realization (the same realization every afternoon) that nothing I do, nothing I think, or worry about, or desire, will last in its seriousness: that from the perspective of a not-even-too-far-off future, the sum of my life will be a small, petty game played by an ordinary man of his time, because you know: my life has been completely uneventful.

Like a bird through the cover of the trees, I cannot arrest you in my thoughts.

It was water-music that Handel wrote to play on the deck of the King's barge as it passed down the river: German flutes, French flutes, violins, basses, but no voice (because the water itself was voice and had no further need of itself) and it's not a contradiction to point out that I've written books of deep feeling: all of my best feelings have gone into my work, but they have not been lived-feelings, except for the feelings I had for you.

Rootless without nutrient, the swell tip of a hollow flower: the sap traveling slowly up from the end of a nerve, and this is what bodies confer (inelegance): like metaphors for milk left out on the counter.

Because my concern for you is a burden: a way of keeping you only for me, and why are we built this way? to endure such loss and sorrow for somebody not even dead, somebody who has always been there, waiting, or not waiting: waiting and not-waiting, both, and—'The pleasure of unhappiness is the only consistent happiness I feel'—

It has never been without some physical relief that I've had affairs, but something has been missing, that fundamental cliché of inner-existence, that missing something that I've been looking for, that I've looked for, that I've found and lost and found again, all the while continuing to look, and continuing to be trapped within my own looking, and what you see taped to the mirror over the bathroom sink is a picture of you when you were eighteen, and it's not there for any reason in particular, and because my wife—'hates coming up here'—and because she never bothered to ask about it and because I never bothered to explain.

(Having kept you dancing like a wave within me).

And I've been called a seditious, cerebral writer, obsessed by questions of loneliness, liberty and guilt: and that's fair, that's true, isn't it? (being unwritten before being written down: being the sound of a consonant inside the mouth (mirror that it is)).

And sometimes I feel like the last man on earth who really loved someone the way I loved you.

White Provence rose-leaves being a bad reason for sorrow (or whatever it was that Richard scattered across the bed the night of your wedding).

Calmly establishing this rapport, this mutual agreement that this is a necessary and final transgression, that each word between us is the last.

Fiction should have a ghostlike presence in it somewhere, something omniscient.

The sentence that orders language to comment on what circles below it.

I've not published a book since my father died.

Noon intersecting with birds and the rhythm of dishes in the cupboard and we'll have to learn how to describe what this is, what we're doing here, and what it will be like if we keep seeing each other, if we form a new habit around ourselves: if we really risk something concrete.

And this tender wave of closeness: your voice in my ear, Mahler's 5th, the adagietto (we heard it in Central Park the last autumn we were together): and this is the memory your touch brings out in me.

The roots of a great love, if deep enough, can retain water and prevent the desertification of the heart.

And this is the material of two complete people passing through the leaves, the soil, the roots of the trees: passing through the tragicomedy of a felt solipsism.

There's an apple orchard down the road and if we keep walking we'll reach it by sunset.

Oh, you, my selfishness, are my desire:

Because everyone dies with their hope still inside of them.

The inner-self is translucent, bloodless: formed from any kind of stone or leaf, because you must know the shape of my hands on your back, the sound of the river in the distance, the sound of the wind in the trees, and—'I'm so incredibly happy Peter'—is all you can repeat to me, over and over:

And New York is always so unlovely, which is why both of us love it, and why we feel the constant need to leave it.

And because character is fate, what happened to us (what you did to me), would happen every time we tried it, and the Greek poets affirm for me a world that is disorderly and passionate: a world that I have never known.

Real life must be the most wonderful novel that nobody has ever read.

Transposing an echo from memory alone, you can be like anyone you want to be, slumped in the grass, laughing at something unbearably funny.

Endlessly—'being shattered and overtaken'—yet not unconsecrated, not unknown, and still, I strain for your beauty.

Torn muslin showering us, stamens of dying flowers, mesmerization for its own sake, the first drops of the awareness that ordinary human beings must contradict themselves for sexual gratification.

Because thinking back to the days before we both really grew up—'assumed our public responsibilities, you know'—we were already reduced to the tautology of being alone inside the instance of another, entirely similar, self.

The milkweed (that you noticed just now growing along the side of the house) I seeded to attract monarch butterflies, which feed on the pollen, which is a poison that does not harm the butterflies, only the predators which want to eat them.

Another picture of You: taking a bath: a lilac-petal, half-hidden in spray and steam.

There is a logic inside of everything, call it DNA, or telos, or the will-to-power, but it's there, like a string quartet played perfectly from memory, and even if the organizing principle of our society is utility, we've still got our own poetry to cherish and create.

And no, I've never looked upon my own intelligence with any kind of fondness: I've wanted to rebel against it, rebel against my own intellectualism, and of course I've failed and become the essence of intellectualism: the aging man in a cottage surrounded by his books, at a distance from the embodied, truly physical life that he has written so philosophically about elsewhere.

Readying yourself, shaking out your hair, your tongue rolling over your teeth: the wind will carry us in every direction like dandelion seeds.

And if I had been less of a public figure, published less, given fewer interviews, shown up for fewer readings, maybe I'd feel some greater sense of pride, but as it is,

I feel that I have constructed an impenetrable artifice around myself, an artifice that has reduced the pleasures of literary creation to the merely perfunctory, the pragmatically necessary, the reputation-maintaining.

Please, please recognize—'that I'm happiest'—in this weekend cottage, away from everyone, writing and cutting the grass, and clearing the rain-gutters, and the first affair I had here was in 1989, because it's easier, obviously (it being so secluded here), and failures are always structural, like sunlight captured on the tongue and lost again with speech.

Suppose there's a theological aspect in being human, and then suppose there's not, and then tell me Mariel: what's the difference?

A generation of broken, impossible woman still bandy about in this house, so call them to order Mariel, open yourself to them in desperation: place your tongue on their hips, trace it along the line of the bone, just as I have done.

This is the gorgeous solipsism of the fall: the belief that we can undo time like a metaphysical knot.

And still, still, your body yields itself up, asks to be discovered: so put your hands in my hands: piece life back together like broken glass, watch the sun mould the season with light—'So that I was flooded and overcome'—yes,

*and the heart is willing, always willing to be abandoned,
and—'You haunted me for so long'—*

*Consider and hear me: we could make this memory come
alive again.*

*These are forgotten (or simply unapproachable)
remembrances: feeling so in love with you that I could
run for ten or twelve miles at a time in Central Park,
when there was a new significance to everything, when
the city itself was infinite, part of the air, not restricted
by the zones and laws that defined it, and even now your
hands open and close just like they used to: like butterfly
wings, beautifully balanced and coordinated for flight.*

I moved back in with my father to write The Dancer, and I don't think you know anything about that time in my life: the two years immediately after you left me for Richard, and too little of your nakedness was hidden from me, I thought, which is why you left me in the first place, and why I had so much to write about.

Fiction should have a ghostlike presence in it because—'it makes it a different reality'—

Wanting to write, of course, like the late Rilke: wanting to tack my language to the center of a white sail out at sea.

—'I write to create something that is better than myself, I think that's the deepest motivation, you know that'— and to overcome my shame at never having suffered, materially, the way other people have.

Taking recourse to a vertical projection on the plane of providential design: trying to explain this moment back to myself in a single, impossible image.

The autumnal consciousness is a wistfulness and when I saw you last year at my reading—'I wanted to touch you like I used to'—

It is much worse to love one's parents than to love one's children (because our children we can expect to outlive us), but a lover is in the middle, a toss-up so to speak, someone whose outlasting us is always painfully in doubt.

Because the burden to remember others is too great for me, and I wish being a writer meant doing something else.

Like the white of ivory keys, the great windows to the house facing south with the sun, and whichever way I turn, softly everywhere, your voice, like a sudden gust of wind—'The first time I found your book I bought two copies: one for me and one for my son'—

My breath gushing upwards in plumes (for I have turned and found you longing at my side) and it was when I found my wife, recently, in the kitchen on her laptop, unable to sleep, that I realized that I had done something very cruel to her: kept her near me without giving myself completely to her, and the life we made together, and morality is not a judgement on action, but rather, a judgement on inaction and inattention.

Splayed over the bed knowing that an awareness of something more profound is rising up from our bodies unseen: parents dead, kids moved away, everything stretching too far into the future to follow, and I've loved it all, given everything I've had (cut flowers, peach-blossoms).

And, I admit, the way I've lived my life has revealed all sorts of inconsistencies about my values and my desires: I know, that is, that I've been swinging perilously between extremes without ever reconciling them or even acknowledging their difference.

The trees tumbling into the Hudson, your self-consciousness less and less apparent, and—'there's such a stubbornness in your love Mariel'—and as I get older, god forbid, even our first letters seem like endings rather than beginnings.

Each of us begs for the power to transform ourselves back to what we were, to what we've always wanted to be: nameless—'and like suns, we'll split apart'—

I slash the envelope open and nothing spills out, no word from the outside, no grace, and—'What did you say to me?'—'That I was faithless to you'—the touch of the sun, caught in the wind and the light, come back to me—'Say again why you are here Mariel'—

'...friends over for drinks talking about our children... everyone accepting the common fiction that our lives have some meaning... no courage, no love, no faith at all—'

'It's an uncanny feeling, I can't describe it Peter, and you know I can't, so stop asking'—

Because half is enough (this kind of love) and half is enough for a life, isn't it? because half is all we have, or less, something infinitely less than half, a molecule, a drop of choice in an ocean of fate—'I would read your books in secret while Richard was gardening or playing with Julian'—

Let's recalibrate life to the windy days of terrible unforeign love, I'm thinking: let's raze the houses, let's rebuild the suburbs into romance.

But then, I find myself back (mentally) with Daisy and the kids in Brooklyn (because who do you think inherited THAT house?) and I can see very clearly the coffee-maker and the juicer and the toaster all laid out neatly on the newly renovated kitchen counter (it's marble now) and I can't help but think that those things (the details of a domestic arrangement) form a permanent membrane (or filter) between the soul and everything else.

We grow inside a life: we grow despite it:

I imagine that my arms, my legs, my lips, my tongue, my cock (these vital instruments of intimacy) are all moved by invisible strings above the stage, and I do not ask who moves the strings, or what stage I am on: only that I am controlled from the outside:

How easy it was to be crushed inside this thing called life, called family, called hope, and how easy it was without you, and how impossible.

And Nietzsche's later philosophy came from notebooks he kept while walking, and his aphorisms were really pictures of his thoughts as they rose like bubbles in a pot of boiling water: and I'd like to write like that (and maybe I will).

The trees shaking in the wind, and I feel life (the magma of unconsciousness) pass through me, and because you experience anger as loss I wonder how I can possibly console you Mariel.

Smatterings of blackbirds and finches picking at unity of life, the total entropy of (all) creation, and it's so hard to imagine you and your family (because you are still a symbol for something else to me).

And we shouldn't presuppose that love is present.

And I'm thinking that THIS IS IT, this is my life, the sum of it, the pinnacle of its otherwise forgettable existence in space and time, and I've tried so hard to write good books, good poems, and to be a good father, a good husband, and even though I know that I've 'done my best' when I actually say THAT out loud, it feels like the vaguest excuse, like an attempt to establish an ethic I never actually believed in: because all of this accomplishment, and growth, and maturation has never meant as much to me as the opened-flower of your sex, your breath, your perfect helplessness, because I've always been merciless in caring for that single emotion, the emotion of You, and because you got to the bottom of a color and discovered it was violet (or so you told me) and because I told you that you were like no one else I'd ever met, and because the deconstruction of life is something sacred: my shoulders pushing you against a tree, my hands pulling off your dress, our hands against the heads of the flowerstalks, our mouths turned up to the sky.

The conceptual construction of Us wrapped around us like a blue sweater: everything in mutation, metastization, change, evolution, decay, and the language inside the brain mimics the patterns present in the nature around it: wind, water, dissolution, decay.

Like the one time I raised my hand (it must have been years ago) to strike Daisy: overwhelmed as I was by her submissive, mothering care for me (and of course I put my hand down).

And along with conversation goes the love of words for their own sake and a desire to manipulate them and it's not a matter of intelligence: some very intelligent and original people don't have the love of words or the knack to use them effectively.

There are so many movements inside this one-motion act.

Ours is a vision like a tumbling dice that you might want to see all the sides of at once, but can't, being outside of the gamble itself.

'Don't look at me like that'—'Like what?'—'Like THAT'—

Eat your own leaves, lose your fruit, leave yourself withering in the yard.

I want to form a heart inside the heart.

This is just an instant of fullness before everything is reduced to the margin of its subject: music in the living room, sunlight branching under the door, and the vanity of seeing myself as you see me:

And it must be visible even for those who passed at a distance, like the smallest part of that endless scale, and life runs underneath us like a stream, and I want to fall through myself into the air, and accomplish this for me, the realization of a purely visual mode of sensual appreciation, because when you talk Mariel, sound retakes its place inside the ear (a bobbled tango, a salient hymn) and cudgle me like a slave, put your lips on my tongue, and what is this for, except for freedom?

That whole fissure of light (our creation) is a shattering, and now you're repeating Schubert's last words back to me—'Is there not a place for me on this earth?'—

Forever, in the sense that the household gods have been forgotten, that the retrievable has become the irretrievable (this distance at the point of nearness) and what I really really really want to know Mariel, is, are you still open to what is shining, intact, visible inside of you?

Primarily elegiac: the function of poetry inside this room.

And it passes so naturally you don't realize—'You never understand the security Richard gave me...'—'Because forgetting happens without terror'—and you're right, it just happens, without terror or anything, wiped from the boards like chalk, almost naively, almost without any will or pretense (the erasure): and it's like a hunger feeding on its own desire for more (this unique human desire to be consumed from within).

Deliberately you would unclasp the black pearl from between your teeth in a show of mourning for love.

And part my tongue along the disjunction of suffering please before it is too late.

But do not think that being centered within yourself is a way to resist the feeling of pain or the taste of salt burnt on the tongue.

And during the experience you're not particularly interested in words, because the experience transcends words and is quite inexpressible in terms of words, but afterwards all you want is a feast of language.

We only need to see again through our hearts and hands:

And we are full of forbearance because to hope means to be alone, and because it means to translate personal unhappiness into a final, more alien, unknown.

Cutting oneself down from a position halfway up a piece of dangling rope: all of one's strength is necessary for this, the cutting down.

I like the danger of undressing ourselves in the sunlight, and of you, grinding yourself into the mud and grass like an animal in a storm, and we imagine that we may pass like trees into the ground of time: sink our hands like roots into the softness of the bed.

—'Julian was a responsibility... and for the first time I wasn't selfish... you have to understand how important that was to me, Peter'—

Responsibility being a forwards glance towards our own view of the lives we've lived, a sense of the mistakes we've made, failed virtues, failed ideals of self, and parenthood and family, and how seldom ungathered, these, my sheaves of flowers, and how seldom I feel thrilled anymore, for the life that is ahead.

Pity turned to ink: spilled across the page:

OK, I'll admit it: everything we say to each other is a love poem:

Your sweater, the white wool of it, pulled half over your head one afternoon in Central Park, as you try to kiss me, your classmates laughing at you from the toepath.

Bruised flesh and lilacs in full color, dying off now.

You're so fond of setting our psychic states side by side that you make a chain out of them, but why can't we just relate to each other as separate selves instead of being planets determined to alter themselves with moons? and nothing is ever clear or precise in person and slowly, I realize, I am no longer passionate enough for you.

After a while, we will become just another affair: this is what we're both thinking.

Fear nothing, necessity cuts my wings, and a multitude of sweet flower petals are dead and dry in the grass, and we've got to (re)accept each other, obviously, because the zinnias, tigerlillies, heavy roses are only temporary while winter is real, and this is all in Shakespeare, you know, because it's literature which lends my reality its mass.

A coffee cup with a very dark blue stripe around the rim, a fresh, fully ripened lemon: an entire household of objects to bind oneself to.

And if vulnerability and fear are involved, it is no more than a mild concern that one day it (the heart) will simply stop beating.

We didn't want to be found insignificant under darkening sheets of autumn rain, we didn't want a naked glance to turn into physical ambivalence.

The past wends between our legs like a stray cat, and I don't know what these intense, unpatterned thoughts reveal.

And what gathers us in and what reaps us like wheat, Mariel?

Every sound, every grain of light seems divine to me, your mother's memory, my mother's voice, a chord of life, a piano lieder.

After the breast cancer you weren't the same, as you were saying…

And we can agree that the body-flower sways and shines without moving, that a hand is light when the artist guides it, clasping and circling around the subject, which is its own interiority, and that no one understands this: that light is something that one may carry across a field of darkness: that what we are indifferent to we cultivate, and that what we are indifferent to we reconfigure as a lyrical absence.

Both of us undoubtedly much more sensitive than most people to the general beastliness of things and much more indifferent too.

And to some extent you can relive the experience, particularly the transformation of the outside world: you get hints of this, you see the world in this transfigured way now and then: just not to the same pitch of intensity (but something of the kind).

Reaping the stars fallen on the lawn, letting life pile up gently around us, walking through the late afternoon, your fingers threading the dying flowerheads (the calyx inside the buds):

The leaves are changing, the air is cool, and the sunlight coming through the window catches the steam rising from our tea-mugs.

228

And our (sexual) failure highlights the problems associated with our perception of time as a line, and our reliance on metaphor to understand or describe the feeling of its passage.

—'An affair with a neighbor. Later a co-worker. Then the father of Julian's best friend'—

You didn't know me as a child waking to the sound of my parents talking downstairs, the smell of my father lighting his pipe, sitting down at the typewriter, the smell of coffee and eggs and toast, the autumn leaves rustling in the gutters, the sound of my mother making a phone call, my father receiving friends, the seasons revolving, carrying me like a ferris wheel through time:

And my poems now don't satisfy me because they all seem like constructions without meaning, or maybe that's too simple or too unfair, but I don't really care: what my poems should have been is what you were, and what people should know about me is that I loved you, not that I wrote this-or-that stupid book, and that once, we sat in silence, and talked about growing old.

—'I couldn't sleep with Richard again after this… I can't even imagine speaking to him'—

And I'm not comparing you with anyone except who you were and I'm calling going to call this what it is: a day without consumption, or terror, a day of moving through a few well-lit rooms searching for the distance inside of ourselves, because—'I called you my poet and I always will Peter'—

More and more Mariel, my world, my culture, my life, my home becomes resistant to the simple, the good, the attentive, and more and more any sense of natural wholeness gives way to a state of permanent anxiety and distraction, to the game of maintaining one's reputation, giving interviews, lectures, signings: playing the part of a poet who no longer can write any poems, of a novelist whose only novel is about a woman whose love he was not poet enough to keep.

The body goes unbroken like a chord: my lips on your sex, my hands around your back.

Because beauty is a melody one must relearn again and again, and because, when I run my hands across your chest, I feel a landscape of suffering.

But then to repeat defeats everything: the act of writing is singular, momentary, unstable (or so I want to think).

I'm too much my father's son, too much of an idealist by heart and sympathy, not to be a worried Plato, slipping on after his Forms.

Our creation, our shattering, our desire for music without object, for object without desire at all, and my whole self is given over to this strangeness: the strangeness of you.

And I will lift the love out from you like ore from the mountains.

Emotions that I can't shake off like water from a raincoat:

It is like poetry: how you unknit the body into something strange.

None of this matters (the ontology of touch), the meaninglessness of matter converging and decoupling, the afternoon merging into red hues, orange hues, yellow horizons.

The sycamores are threatening to die again this year, and Time shudders, waiting for Order to put everything back in its place.

She sees with incredible clarity, that's what someone might say about you, but always as though through a sheet of plate glass: she never touches anything.

The afternoon in the hospital hallway the day my father died I overheard a surgeon describing an operation and suddenly, then, any thought of the sacredness of human life (the grandeur and mystery of it) was stripped away and I understood the body for what it is: a construction of bones, strings, tubes, and liquids, that you can tinker around with if something inside of it should break.

Your toes curled back, your eyes dead, your smile like crocus mouth.

Like Leda with a swan: one beautiful long last shout.

You have to fight to retain your youth and we didn't.

—'Because I was just some girl who you screwed and never forgot about...'—

The tree-covered banks of the Hudson are turning yellow and the yellows under the cold rain are not increasing gradually, but the next-to-last tones are almost there, and then there will come the falling off of the last leaves, the falling off that begins as if from a great height (out of Nowhere) into the womb of your hands.

Entropy equal to contact, entropy dominating the order of events, the arrival of your car, the opening of the car, kissing in the sun, angry words in the kitchen, the gradual unbalancing of our emotions, tea in the lawnchairs, the path behind the house, wine on the porch, the awareness of an oblique kind of failure.

And look how it falls away from us, our sense of wonder, like leaves of roses—'Richard still loves me'—'After you left me I built my life around a managerial type of domesticity'—a strange verb untensed in the middle of this incredibly musical chord—'is this the same love as before?'—

Each word has an internal texture: each word has the salience of fire: so paint me over the walls, close the circle of my eyes.

I stretch my hand out to you (as if I could make the leaves fall faster from the trees)—and your desire assimilates me into a void, the void and form of you (your wings extended over the surface of a single autumn afternoon) and it is a shape I almost fail to recognize: not having seen you for so long.

Observe the nomenclature of light, describe it, make note of it, and listen closely to the murmur of the season, and realize that consciousness, like nature, is underwritten by faith: unbounded and unlimited by the rules that make The Self comprehensible, and perhaps it (Love) comes from Christianity, or something long before then, and there is also the idea of a lost paradise in Hindu culture too, and complaining about a headache you say you have to be—'getting back to the city'—and, well—'alright Mariel, alright'—

Because Life removes itself from the kernel of the deeper, lonelier life, and it is not only other people, who you open towards, but the possibility of life among them, as a part of them, unconscious and gifted with impossibility of the death: it is just how we give ourselves to each other, and how we are afraid, but how we may still love (how we may still create).

(It is like you have become a wound: a wound as pointed as the final, moral wound itself (the wound of separation)).

IV. Allegretto poco mosso

past midnight driving to the shore with the windows open imagining olive groves and white houses under dark-leaved lemon trees dog stars laying panting at the edge of the water the salt air in our teeth

NOTEBOOK OF PW [6.6]

Greekblue, seablue—open Your eyes; what we're waiting for (to unconceal ourselves).

The hearth-ache again (this theme of returning).

and One imagines you anointing the scars of an ocean One imagines you closing the valves of your throat with a wrench (it is an unaccounted-for sweetness a sheer depth that terrifies me) voice after voice day after day and have you been there before? could you tell me what it is like?

NOTEBOOK OF PW [6.7]

The ferry arrives as the sun is setting. Feeling uncertain—

Listening to the darkness like a seashell.

Peter opening up the front door the ferry lights visible out at sea

his soft way of speaking (the chest voice) consonants softly breaking still so strange in the ear thinking: we've done it

NOTEBOOK OF PW [6.8]

Inner resources:
The flash of salt in the sea-glare;
The flesh of her palms pressed
Her lips, quietly—against my cheek.

I hear the winds rake its fingers across beech bark;
stripping it of its rough skin.

And now?—the shadow of the white sand. Our exhaustion. The breath of the water whitely blooming over us; and the dark sea rising—flower by flower, rising. Black-blue, translucent, rolling on the wake of snapping foam—our fingers linked like the leaves of an all-white sea-anemone; our fingers picking at pieces of white glass washed on the beach; our fingers pinching the nerves behind our eyes—turning the evening into darkness.

M is reading Marguerite Duras and has been smiling for two straight days. I don't think she wants to be bothered by anyone, including me.

my body like a ruined pillar sunk in the harbor

nuzzling my head against his shoulder like a child or a dog the dumbness of a gesture: my holding the door open for him (him crying while cutting onions on the counter straining what other means are left to us in our peril)

a bush growing close in the dunes a salt flood a shoreline in the process of erosion

NOTEBOOK OF PW [6.10]

We drink the local tea, stare out the window at the sea.

In the wind: nameless. The stars noting well
The common ideation of love,
Remunerated according to intricate desire.
Because language decides what it is.
How people fix a way of thinking
Like a rope tied around the waist.

The dining table here always seems to bear a jug of homemade red wine and dishes made from garden vegetables... Small goat herds make their presence known with their bells.

I feel painfully ill at-ease.

and we don't want kindness we want our own world: our own bewildering but autonomous breathing world Peter

or do we? I'm so prone (already!) to doubling back on my
own assertions questioning them until they admit that
they were lies to begin with

NOTEBOOK OF PW [6.10]

How distant the touch, the smell of her; how
profoundly difficult this is—embodying antithetical
tendencies; pouring through the universe like water.

Neither of us willing to enforce the rule of 'brutal
honesty' that we set for ourselves. Not that we've
ever been—

The island is mountainous for the most part. I like
drinking the local tea and watching the sea at night.
I am reminded of Milton's phrase 'symphony of
stars'.

There are types of blue, M says, that are unimaginable
until you've been to the Mediterranean.

It is only for love that I grasp
You by the hair: pull you through
The moonlight like a dream.

My emotional life is so contracted, so muted, so
compressed that I do not assent, even privately, to
the idea of pain—

Her speaking voice gathers itself around me like a
sea of mud, waves lapping—

Forgetting home has proved difficult for both of us.
And yet—that smile of hers; spread like a fragrance
everywhere.

A knife, halfway in the water.
A stone carried away in the wind.
A summer without discipline.
An ecstasy, a gloaming.
Endurance. Adoration.
Perhaps we are, but it is
Only flesh.

There are thermal springs, east and west of the main
port, I learned today.

NOTEBOOK OF PW [6.11]

The craning birds choose you:
Their plumes black, their beaks
Snipping open your pearlshell skin.

'Peter you know I'm not shocked by sex anymore,'
M says.

The stars we sheared from the night:
These are the playthings that I kept for you:
Your eyes undark, your navel arched.

In the mental scene, I escape out the doors of silence—and like an infant fist, she opens, reaching after me.

A cut, then dissociation.
A cut: then the pandemonium of curiosity and Self-awareness.

I want my past to evaporate like rainwater in the warm sun. We both do.

NOTEBOOK OF PW [marginal commentary]
The metaphysical tide.

A fish hooked through the gills—the black shoals of muscle and organ exposed.

The leak is in the language—

Unwritten books, unwritten loves: both are consequences of my passionate lack.

There is no interpretation of literature: only our immersion in it.

Odysseus might have preferred to die with the sirens before reaching Ithaka.

Criticism ought learn to call bad books bad and good books good; and this is NOT a tautology or obvious statement—because our language resists; pushes us backwards.

Demanding that a book hew close to the 'concrete' is an evasion of literature's inherent metaphysics.

Poetry is concentration, silence, internalization: poetry removed from these practices is just artificial language.

how could we become unburied again? pass back into the daylight? (the question of the Greeks who reside in the underworld)

(because I have so many restless questions today that Peter gives answers to that make no difference at all internally for me because he has not really thought about them (his answers/what I'm feeling))

but was Richard any different? I can't recall

(men being all the same I guess)

NOTEBOOK OF PW [6.12]

We are undivided between physical violence and physical love.

243

There is something here that is comparable to the experience of suspension, inaction, reverie.

There is always a transference from the visual to the verbal.

And why this feeling of falling-off?—of a nadir—of despair—?

The beginnings of a novel today. But only for the sake of having something to do this summer—I have no deeper ambition—

'Why does our society value love so much?' M asks as we are getting ready to go to bed. 'Because it doesn't,' I respond.

Have been rereading Kafka the past few days—appreciating his gnostic humor—his playful ghostliness—

Fragmentary language—language of the heart—I've given something precious up—the same thing I always give up, over and over.

We cannot delve under rock and
Flourish forth with the manifold of
Necessity and spiritual love.
Aporia means that one does not make it to

The end, that one breaks off midflight
And plummets into the remainder of
The earth:

NOTEBOOK OF PW [6.14]

This is our process of invisible completion—
escaping to the sea—the sea which is our lost love; a
dense black cloud; a single silhouette—numbed into
hypnosis...

Don't mince experiences

Or words.

Waves generating silence from the cloud; clouds
from the sea; a single figure waltzing on the sand.

Crazily, M. says we should stay here and adopt a
child (believing that we are not too old). She cites
Wordsworth's poem Michael in support of her
argument.

The waves gather, like birds pleading for morning.
Her bones are made of midnight.

A small cluster of dots are placed together without
touching: this is the impression of longing I drew
in my sleep.

We've begun to mimic each other, she points out to me, in the way that husbands and wives often do— and she's right.

And down the path to the garden,
Rosemary clinging to the stones,
I go to bury you, Eros.

Then I think that she is like a perfect book; one whose pages have never been cut—like a bird's folded wing or a fan never opened:

Fragments of an unwritten, halfwritten novel: the work growing through the latticework of our bodies.

'Write about this man who, drop by drop, squeezes the slave's blood out of himself until he wakes one day to find the blood of a real human being—not a slave's—coursing through his veins.' (Chekhov)

A woman spinning in the doorframe.
Pain, she says, nearer to the heart.
Pain you say, but you don't know where.

'My soul is a can of condensed milk,' she tells me, as she undresses in front of the window.

The way she describes Richard makes me think that she never gave him a chance—

Youth cannot be recovered—that a door is shut, locked behind us—

Poets lie.

But poems—poems are ropes we tie around our waists before we leap into the void. (And some days I remember that lightness is an act of daring.)

The gables of the houses; a fading road below a blue sky studded with stars. Darkblue or violet with a green tree: a painting of a night without black. She spreads around me like an ocean—kissing me on the ear, the neck; telling me to come to bed.

I had a philosophical system; she ripped it in half like a pillow; sent the feathers flying—

Blue as glass:
Murex shells,
Spiralling away
From the anthropology
Of hope.

Discipline (attention) being the true mode of prayer.

We don't need to explain ourselves; after all—
Shakespeare didn't.

*no language but a cry so careless this single life of ours
Peter*

*you are someone who is constantly representing yourself
as the medium through which you speak while I am just
myself in my own form*

*but desperately desperately I want to go home sometimes
(want to see my son) and I feel this has been a mistake
and writing does not make it better (this mistake)*

*and just now he comes in the door with a fish he's caught
grinning ear to ear ready to fry it in olive oil and me not
knowing what to say to him because he's so incredibly
pleased with himself*

*pleased with himself above all for not being Richard and
for never having been anything like him*

*my own face looking backwards through the fatal webbing
of his hands of salt air and cigarette smoke (of June nights
bleached and left out to dry in the wind)*

*and listen! the moon is like an animal howling wounded
behind the clouds*

*he passes through me a wave of blood rising through the
lungs (rising through me like sap through the stems of
trees)*

Together, we talk about living by the water, smoking handrolled cigarettes, eating fish for dinner; about the shore blanched by sunlight—crushed like a grape in the evening; about purer, more Ionian evenings intersecting with half-sublime nights; about our bodies bleached and dried out like the bones of whitefish in the sun; about our drinking coffee with goat's-milk, late at night—

Black-tongued; the sea like a forest on fire.

There is no literature apart from the compression of literature: one hears then the full cry of the human.... A book is never in a hurry: it reads us from within as we read it from without....

I feel as if the more superficial I get, the better access I have to profound and weird relationships among words. In this sense I think I agree with Nietzsche that what made the Greeks profound was their unabashed superficiality. Language can only deal meaningfully with a special, restricted segment of reality; the rest—and it is presumably the much larger part—is unheard of; silent; at-rest.

The intervention of physical force is
To mandate intellectual loss, or fear.
The rain clears the air in June. Open

The windows in all the rooms.
The original vacancy deepens:
'Hoi polloi, goodbye.'

The soul resists tautology by remaining alive.

No renew, only decay. No decay, only renewal. I can't decide.

It is ourselves we return to whenever we return home: it is Us waiting at the door.

Insult without reason: that I do not always want her.

Tomorrow, we'll watch old women with paper-roses languish in their beach-chairs and we'll realize how mutable the sea is—how it has less shape than even we have... and the next day we'll spend a clear blue afternoon not getting out of bed—listening to the sea like a string quartet outside our window.

Talking about our children, our plans, our aging bodies; saying goodnight; collapsing sunburnt into bed.

She talks about Richard more than I talk about Daisy.

Sexual disgrace.
A dress lifted over

The head. Summer comes fast:
It bullies the flowers.
And because you love me,
You tell me that
You are a friend of mine.

Shakespeare, Blake, Keats—the only poets who were
in love with love. (Goethe was only pretending).

And don't think that I forget what her body used
to be—spun like silk between my fingers—because
time is stored up in our bodies, stored up in our
touch; we are like granaries overflowing with wheat.

Wings, decorative like pearls.
Bees in the window.
Strawberries for lunch,
O' my love.
Magically, all things.
(Dissolve).

Gap-toothed and lean as a dog—I find her waiting
for me.

And the imagination has two colors: blue and green.
And rosebright, she folds back into me; back into
our bed with the sun going down. And more and
more, our elopement seems unreal.

(Enchantment/Disenchantment).

It is a shame Nietzsche died before Einstein's theory
of relativity.

Because we are
All constantly gathering ourselves
Around you, pulling you within the
Bitter framework of our arms.

The old white houses that leave an impression on
the skin of the eye: consciousness is expanded and
pushed upon from the center out.

I would pluck the flowers
That grow from the ruined shell of you,
Broken on the floor.

Animals mourn, fish, birds; the trees mourn; the
marshgrass mourns; the sea mourns.

White branches, blue leaves: the night spreading its
fragrance, and the scent of almonds, and the rain,
and the sea, not far off.

Realizing: this is the part of the body rooted to
Death.

Mothers and daughters talk
On the telephone.

The voices change and stories pull themselves
Into a narrative of
Unspoken hope.
Later, the window is
Shut like an eye stung by salt.
Chairs and sofas are put back
Into order.

when was it when we rented the shorehouse for two weeks? I think I was twenty I remember floating in the water like a piece of driftwood: I remember laying sprawled in the sand: blackened by the sun: my skin dry with salt

other memories now too: my father reading in a beach-chair: my mother giving me a plastic bucket and shovel

a world that begins to resemble the shape of his tongue wrapped around a word (the shape of a vowel dying in his throat) and I'm not just talking about screwing each other: I'm talking about the full gradient of intimacy and closeness: the total sweetness the total whatness of one physical presence (mine) nested inside the other (his):

and no and not even like when we were younger but NOW while we are ungathering ourselves piece by piece NOW while we are sharing our own sweat and lust and heaviness with one another NOW while we are conscious of having a NOW to share

the wind gone slow and still the wake foaming pale blue
sweetly inside our cupped hands curdwhite moments
of tenderness bunched together like violets or drops of
searain or like almonds scattered against a windshield

NOTEBOOK OF PW [6.17]

Open my guts; open my navel with your cleaning
knife; thread a shining fishing-line through my
cheeks—

The only responsibility a writer has is to avoid moral
and emotional death.

Tell me that life is open-ended, incomplete, almost
infinite.

Human and inhuman—physical grief:

Werther being the young Goethe himself, minus the
creative gift.

The copper of the
Old phone
Line is like
A nerve:

Strings and atoms and quarks (all brightly
quivering)—

A certain distance in time is absolutely necessary for a novelist, unless he is writing a journal.

Yet: I *am* my characters and their world.

When my son was 17, he forgot to flush a condom down the toilet, and my wife found it—to her horror. It seems to me that family life is regulated by sexual shame: that the values which prevent and constrain adultery are the same that constrained Mariel and I when we were young.

We like members of an uncollected tribe, sitting around a fire for the first time in a generation.

And bittersweet (in Greek—'Eros the bittersweet') bittersweet because we cannot separate pleasure from pain; bittersweet because our bodies are cut in half like flatfish.

Before beginning a novel I recreate inside myself its places, its milieu, its colors and smells.

You were the pathic one, because you
Felt everything you received.
The pieces of my hands.
The fragments of my teeth.
And what does anybody know?
(Because the house is filling up with water).

NOTEBOOK OF PW [marginal commentary]

Nothing that I could not fling like glass against a wall and break—

everything is subjective radiant lyrical

imitation roses and something about a kind of Hindu strangeness that infuses us when we die

blushed to annihilation so I am willing to go along no beginnings or ends only transitions

NOTEBOOK OF PW [6.21]

Mercy never being easy; the flash of expression in her eyes—'Peter!'—almost unbearable—

In the harrowing, I will reconceive of
You, I will pull the skin of language
Over your tongue, sew it shut.

My grandmother was Hungarian, and I still remember, more than anything, the smell of paprika in the hallway of her apartment. And that's what life is, I think: the smell of paprika in the hallway.

Salt to the ocean, sweetness to the flower; riding my bike for hours today—to clear my head, or just to be alone; to be alone probably.

A trip tomorrow to see the local ruins. According to local custom, there are still marble statues embedded in the sand off the coast.

An anxiety: have I become indifferent to her?

Aim at the mediated void,
Spreading over us like a bleached,
Billowing sheet: under the surface
Of this erasure-mark the eye
Feels as if it has been
Bruised for good.

said he would join me on the porch tonight to watch the stars fall but no he stayed inside reading as usual and so it's up to me to watch them (the stars):

strong clean soporific my eyes turned inward oblivious to his anger

I imagine shoals of plankton swarming along the beach turning the sand pink

black pines waiting for us to fall asleep

NOTEBOOK OF PW [6.21]

A fight—if that's what you call it. Her greeting me with sunburnt eyes; accusing me of something—I almost forget already.

I feel tired, tired, tired—and how could I feel tired
in a place where there is nothing to do but sleep,
and fish, and eat? Normally, I would feel ashamed
... but I'm indifferent to shame as I'm indifferent
to everything else. Or maybe this is just a passing
feeling; maybe, maybe. I'm afraid to write all of this
down—

'You aren't the kind of writer that people will
remember after you're dead,' she said. 'Your only
fans are the women you've slept with.'

Grace is gentle. And
It submits. And you've
Always known it.
(Because you've seen enough
Of it to know).
Dead summer nights and
Imitation flowers.
Love again.
Spoiled child.

No progress artistically, but—?—what else could I
expect? still: I go stir-crazy without work; I cannot
be around another person all day with absolutely
nothing to do; it is less romantic than I remember
it—

The idiom of the eye is communicated back to the hand, the mouth: the whole body, compelling it to TAKE TAKE TAKE.

Aware that she is disappointed in me. A few rude words in the kitchen. Kissing to make up. (We revere make-up kisses).

NOTEBOOK OF PW [6.23]

The night is heavy with darkness; ripe like a grape— one must stamp one's feet on it; churn the juices in a vat; store the night away; let it ferment.

Examine the metaphysical
Purpose of a fractal.
A poem like this is its own sequence:

What takes place during sex is a sort of crystallization around the person. It is quite indescribable.

I go down to the rocks to collect driftwood; the sea is terrifying at night. I imagine myself, my own eyes: empty, flooded—

inviting and sweet the dawn waiting for us to open our eyes Peter

because you'd like to break me like a scarlet flower across

your knee watch the red run down around my ankles fuck
me like a dog draw out the blood of the heart

the salt issued of the sea like a tear (acrid Venus begging
at your knees)

NOTEBOOK OF PW [6.24]

The sea at night is tremendously blue even without
light; the sea is like Chopin at the piano—the white
keys pouring over themselves in waves; the black
keys riding across the tops white ivory—and her
fingers are very white, like the fingers of her mother
who loved to play the piano—very badly and very
emotionally, as I recall.

NOTEBOOK OF PW [marginal commentary]

Now: the moon's astonished eyes—

Translucency:

And what a woman delivered yesterday, she will
deliver today.

And when a woman says that something is beautiful,
she means it. (Because self-expression should affect
the manner of expression).

Hurt back into poetry: the pure mathematics of denial. The art form of 'no'.

A pattern enacts itself along the curve of a wave, sorrow becomes as light as a watercolor.

Nature keeps the process of generation ongoing, like an electric factory along the highway.

A thin concept conceals an ideal bloom:
Take a blue image, immerse it in a radiance, enroll
The negative at the Imperial School Of Ballet.

And there is no stronger form of discipline than 'yes'—then a letting-be.

Her white teeth—I feel her breasts, her hips in the dark.

At the break between chest and headvoice.
Happiness is not wrong.
Brandnew carnation.
Nine months, never having floated
For that long before.

I do not know how to answer my own youth: the question of my own hope.

Summer and fall have nothing to look forward to. The only two optimistic seasons are winter and spring.

For fear to wake her; softly; gentle patience in the night. Like a musician lingering on a sadnote; harsh and heavy; the impression of her body on the mattress altered.

Allusive, delicate in her knowingness. And god, what have we been waiting for but this?—this difficult poetry of touch—

NOTEBOOK OF PW [marginal commentary]

Caught a fish today, let it go. (See Blake on eternity).

Apart from the voice,
One speaks and sheds briefest flower;
A bird cries.
Then: rejuvenating rain.

NOTEBOOK OF PW [6.26]

The heavy sound of breakers—wind rattling like a bag of stones.

Intricately, like laced hands,
It returns through
You as a poem. But you have waited.

And how inhuman it feels:
Praying for its return.

I remember that when my tonsils were taken out in the first grade, the anesthesia didn't work very well, and I woke up just slightly enough to think: 'I'll not get to finish the book Dad got me as a present for when I wake up!'

A thousand bluewhite flowers scattered over our graves; bluewhite flowers sending their roots through our bodies, down; a hand waves in the dark—

NOTEBOOK OF PW [marginal commentary]
I am buried in light up to my shoulders.

Underneath Chopin is the counterpoint of Bach—

I have lost all confidence in the speaking voice—I will not let it free.

it's someone else's youth now: someone else's porcelain darkness: someone else's thread of pearl:

and there were sarabandes of mutual (incommensurable) longing: pirouettes of burning (metaphysical) flowers

NOTEBOOK OF PW[6.27]

A screen of light on the water.

M reads *Antigone* in bed. I am sitting on the porch—
thinking of my father—

A poem means having the strength to bear a wound:
it means that Goethe had no more poems when he
died.

Emotion transferred by separation. She walks
down to the beach. I stay inside reading.

The bowl is polished until the
Ivory shines through you
Like a whisper;
Shines just like Love.

What do you not know by heart you do not love.
What you know by heart you cannot lose to someone
else.

NOTEBOOK OF PW [6.28]

Her exact words this morning: 'I woke up this
morning and the sun was lying like a birthday
present on the table; so I opened it up and so many
happy things went fluttering into the air.'

'Why don't you ever look at me when you're speaking?' (another one of her tropes)

I create a shadow for myself, let it ride a ways out; out to sea.

A cluster of lilacs
Pinned to your vest. It
Always draws the attention
Of others when you walk down
The street: defeats the purpose
Of their admiration.

And we carve it from absence: it is no plentitude.

Will you, phraseless, speak yourself
Back into the moral order
From which you began?
Because this is the real god-function:
This furnishing of world with
Motive and retribution.

Truthfully, I am incapable of doing anything decisive, precisely because I have already done the decisive thing.

The Greek: 'Agnosia': unknowing.

'Why are we still here if we don't love each other anymore?' M asks. 'Or if we never did?'

'I love you.' M says later.

'The painter who is just beginning thinks that he paints from his heart.' (Matisse)

A trench is drawn across
The blind point in your experience:
A synthesis of limitation and flight
Is conceived of: forgotten: lost.

these plumes of the thought that erupt from a depth thoughts that mirror (invert) what is occurring on the surface of my own language

it's about two in the morning or later (I've stopped checking) and I like the night I like the sound of the waves and the sound of planets swimming across space and I feel like I'm holding back a wave of static electricity

because because because : webwork : a million single stars shining

(a resuscitation)

I like the creative silence; no phone ringing—no emails—no computer; nothing to cut the meditative rope thrown perilously into the void; I do not wish to remain in a place where I have neither solitude nor company. I wish only for some pattern to emerge—a series of days that I can call my life.

Your skin is black with oil and milk.
When I catch you,
I will pin your wings to the bed.

If you snip despair at the neck, it will grow two heads in the place of the first. (It is better to let despair alone).

'I'm jealous and I wish that you were jealous too.'

A book is like a vine, climbing around the trunk of an old tree.

Observation: there are no more poetic revolutions.

'I'm not tired of fucking,' she yells at me, 'I'm tired of fucking you.' And this seems fair to me—

And how unlike rain or silence, it is to write a poem.

Your head is drawn down
Over your arched back,
Taught like a ripple of sinew.
Your eyes are black like smoke.

'There is not enough love and goodness in the
world for us to be permitted to give any of it away
to imaginary things.' (Nietzsche)

1.
A theory of pearl
Is meticulous unless
Written down.

2.
Scatter your life
Like apple seed:
Nothingness is real.

3.
And now Summer comes.
Shakespearean clown.
Shell of metaphor.

*like I've been carried on the top of a swell that won't
stop cresting: a swell that falls to a trough that is itself
the peak of another swellcrest: one after another in an
infinite series*

a sense of pain no different than sorrow and yet so unlike sorrow at the same time

Peter's reverent way of condescending to me: the same as it always was (and he remains unaware that I am aware of what he is getting away with)

NOTEBOOK OF PW[marginal commentary]

Autonomy becomes central to ethical decisions. Autonomy is what constructs a human being. What constructs autonomy remains unknown.

There is always a transference from the visual to the verbal: a transference which creates the very possibility of the work becoming a sensible event.

NOTEBOOK OF PW[6.30]

Being in the sun, driving with the windows open—I want to write about that too; I want to remember that happiness TOO—the happiness of coming very close to something fundamental and good.

There is the responsibility of loving oneself, of persisting, in order that one can love others as one loves oneself: I accept that duty, begrudgingly—

HERE is something comparable to the experience of suspension, inaction, or reverie—but what is it?

What each of us understands by the word soul is different. The soul is the fixed point around which we are constructed.

Reading Thucydides as the sun goes down—the rivers, the fields; the tragedy of people—

To aim literature like an arrow at the ship of Death— that is all I've ever wanted to do.

opening the porch doors: letting the night in like guests to a party

birds' bones:

traveling lady stay awhile'

NOTEBOOK OF PW[marginal commentary]
To have love and loss before me like the yolk and shell of an egg.

Being obscure is being someone else.

Rilke once wrote that it was 'seriously and profoundly significant' that one could not hear a nightingale in America.

A self-blossoming: an emergence.

NOTEBOOK OF PW[7.1]

Little adulteress, before we are punished, let's be wonderful together.

NOTEBOOK OF PW[7.2]

This is a clever lie.

Frostbit stars.
Close to hymn.
This is the manifold of
Music, pressed like eggwhites
Against the eyes.

And does this matter? this deftness with untruth?—

Tonight, during dinner, we started laughing, and we didn't stop. We even forgot to finish our meal. The dishes are still on the table.

We could repair the water
Like we were thinking of flowers.
Because you were unlooked for
At the moment you returned to me.

finger on my lip: 'are you angry?' in that not very nice way he has of asking questions

a waste of breath

NOTEBOOK OF PW[7.3]

Her body is a dark flower, radiating from the kernel
of her groin.

NOTEBOOK OF PW[7.4]

It is unbeautiful, the way
You lay there,
Waiting for me to release you.
My fingers in your mouth.

Dark patches on the sea where stars once fell—

Closed pearl, my language
Inside of language. But not a shame-
Virtue, a virtue-virtue.

Love forms around her like a shell—grows more
complicated each day. Sinew stretched across a bow;
an animal skin, laid across a drum.

Narcissus flowers in her hair—

Like a tongue in the seamud—this moral pain—

An insect moves
Along the inside of a teacup.
A Child breaks open the image inside
An earthenware jar.

Two strangers, kissing, being near, barely touching—I want to describe this unutterable feeling:—the burden of being loved by other people; of being needed by them.

When my mother died I gave that feeling up—or: I thought I gave it up.

Bend in close to me
Like the wind. Emerge from
The shunning of my voice:

Humbly, I am asking you to
Fall with me through
Our passion.
Shuffle sideways: spread your wings.
Music: stop.

A stone wall has physical strength. So does the eye. So does a blade of grass.

Funny how neither of us have any friends to have call on us here. Or friends worth asking to do so—

Being, breath (Shakespeare, Dante)—I am split in two.

A strand of poetry like cut hair
Falling over the pillow.
Lips kissed back,
Salt forming on the windows.
His thumb on her lips:

Like an exotic in Gaugin—purples and yellows—
flowers in her hair—breasts heavy with rainwater.

I should go to sleep. I might read—I don't know
what I want to do.

A picture of a mutilated statue of Hercules with no
head or limbs on the desk.

The lineage of motion is gesture:
Reference to a world
Without future:

Sometimes I think that my books have only made
things worse for me—that they have given people
this sense of access to me that simply doesn't exist.

And yes: I think this is the reason she tries to tunnel
into me; tries to dig a channel under the sea, island
to island—mind to mind.

Old woman take their place
In the order

Of things. Death stands us
On our heads.
Dispose the world in categories.
We are who we are.

NOTEBOOK OF PW [marginal commentary]

Pascal reminds me: the sphere of finesse is not that
of geometry—

The beach is beautiful at night: a tentative,
Uncertain beauty.
Held like a wounded bird
In the hands, this light.

for every early bud a threatening frost in our house at the
base of the mountains

weeping romantically preparing to write another
masterpiece and I can only roll my eyes

but nothing gets lost if you say nothing about it

NOTEBOOK OF PW[7.6]

We have only this dismay: our obligation.

Where do our stars come from?
And where does our water begin?

We could sit around talking like this
For hours. (And we do).

I want to crawl back under the covers of the dark.

Do not take me in so close.
Do not say that anything is best.
Do not say that I am the best.
Windburned, lips parted.
Do not say it.

I was so spiteful today with her. But I am alright
with that.

*yes the stars glistened then and yes they were like
fragments of glass or sand and yes and we scattered them
across field of vision and yes I married someone else*

*and yes I surrendered my life to Him and He is awful
awful awful impossible asking me for everything at once
assuming the remainder of my presence on collateral or
something I don't know!*

*and He is everywhere all the time and this house is far too
SMALL but it is all I could ever want it is inconceivable
(my wanting something else)*

*AND LOVE like a naked girl bathing in the sea: the old
gods crying from the waves for joy*

*this minor but radical disruption of thinking in a straight
line (from Peter to Richard to Peter) the summer almost
ending or not quite ending but being halfway done already*

*everything out of polish and spit and why won't he tell me
anything about the affair he's having in afternoons when
I'm out bathing because I would understand or maybe I
wouldn't but that's not the point no the point is that we
agreed to be fundamentally honest and we have not been*

*the point being that maybe there is no such thing as
honesty only the freedom of taking pleasure in the lie*

NOTEBOOK OF PW [7.8]

You, rising moon, look after us.

Rose-in-hand; sea-rose. Threadbare as anything.

Listening means
Contest: it means: agon.

A letter from my son: no one else thinks enough of
me to write. But how can I blame them?

Rain dishevelled darling.
Dancer, tangoist.

Bearing a vessel on my shoulder this whole summer;
wanting to toss it over the sea-cliffs.

Your hair
Strewn with seaweed.
But no more talking about it:
That's what we agreed.

Thinking: my son is nothing like I was. And: should
I be relieved?

A clay urn of
Practical consideration.
Plague yourself with flesh.

I'm aware she's happier being thought of more as
my lover than as my wife. But then again, she is
so jealous of Daisy and will never admit it; maybe
because Daisy is younger and because she is loyal to
me in a way that M. never has been.

Let the light of the
Body out.
The play has ended.
A new nomenclature speaks.
The earth foists you up like a flower:
You'll drink from a paper-cup.

lamp swinging over the beach our voices hushed summer
evenings on the porch the glow of daylight disintegrating
into blackness (I remember those) and his eyes (darkdraped
over his upturned mouth) opened again to mine and I

may see through them revealing (unconcealing) his light
in each one of its cinema frames

thalassa thalassa:

we turn we turn around we go forward we collapse in
the tide:

we tie for first to see the sun because we always wake up
together

graceful and green as a stem

NOTEBOOK OF PW [7.9]

Death is closed off to us like a house inside a house,
a house without any windows or doors.

You tugged the moon down from
Heaven with your teeth clenched,
And your eyes open.

Love is always an intellectual project.

The transformation into an artist is always reversible
because courage can always return to fear.

Language, without a set theory of its
Own function, functions.

But I do not depend on the
Colorless fiction of doubt:

The two of us drinking wine in the kitchen after
dark—

In the guts of the flowers,
That which you call the smallest seeds.

Bloom:
Dead River. Black
Water. Run like music.
Uncreative. Above
All Things.

NOTEBOOK OF PW [marginal commentary]
Caught up in the drama of salvation.

'If you are afraid of loneliness, don't marry,' Chekhov
wisely advised.

NOTEBOOK OF PW [7.11]
I remember what I can't deny (no record of action
no caring for anything but this):—a love to fill a
void; but a love too—yes—that became a void—

Yes, You, my heart: I remember You.

'No, if my suffering could be cured by such means it would not be serious... I ask you with what energy remains to me at the end of this letter: If we value our lives, let us abandon it all.' (Kafka, Letter to Felice, November 11th, 1912)

As softly as desire: wave after wave: her mouth closing over mine:

We hurl ourselves against ourselves. We are like two stones ground down to dust.

Erotic flattery is the most obvious and reductive pleasure in the world and I, unwisely, do not refuse it.

Her hair has grown long, like fallen rain.

After a month here, our skin has begun to glow from the salt and sun. And of course, we indulge ourselves in the myth of youth.

We want to stand on open ground. And we want to look everywhere and see open space and move across it.... And so there is this question of perspective:

A writer must be an enchanter, not a craftsperson, a trinket-maker.

Nothing is antithetical to the rules that govern literature: a real, that is living, literature absorbs

everything into its chaotic yet fundamentally
coherent substructure—language.

And no one can stand to look at you,
Dancing across the bare floors in
Your white, Tolstoyan dress.

The July moon hung like a painting on the sea.

Stars hiss into the water. I plunge after them like a
fisher-bird:

What I am against is this terrible lie that there is too
much great literature to read in a lifetime. Actually,
there is very little; enough to read in a year; much
that is interesting, little that is great.

*some very particular emotion crystallized all too perfectly
inside a text like a tiny refracting mirror and be so moved
as to be completely undone by it*

*but then again I learned everything from being so
unhappy and my life might have turned out even more
banally than it has without it (that feeling)*

still the moon shares nothing with you:

*summer advancing like an army with the initiative of
surprise:*

brushed onto the darkness like a painted star

and whatever love I have been able to mine from the
under the surface of whatever ordinary emptiness my
world is sometimes defined by is due to that very precious
understanding of what it means to want to die not in the
grandiose sense of wanting to be annihilated but in the
quiet sense of wanting to discover the other side of the
particularly metaphysical face of pain

because the earth breathes for us and because the earth
is our flower and because tears spring from the bones in
our throats and because it was Aristotle (Peter explained)
who rarely mentions forgiveness

missing the theater which I promised him would not
happen but it's happening

NOTEBOOK OF PW [7.12]

The sea like a city with the power out—tufts of
white uncarved beech trees.

The stars are minor-key compared to the music of
pure thinking.

How earnest people become
When you crush them into suffering.

I've planted a little vegetable garden in the back of
the cottage. We eat arugula salads for dinner now
with fish. I have not felt so healthy in years. The

diet and exercise create the illusion that it is her love that is restoring my youth. 'You look fantastic Peter … even I look fantastic,' she exclaims.

Having to wake up, pace around, smoke a cigarette, make coffee, let it grow old: unable to go on with the novel I knew I wouldn't be able to go on with when I came here. But I have nothing to prove at my age.

Drawing on the same sources—Rilke, Kafka, Beckett….

Herbal tea with goat's milk, cigarettes again. The lamp on the table. I'll miss this only when I'm back at home—

And later the gathering of sea-lilies—the two of us alone on the beach with the exception of an old man who has walked down here from the village.

Not saying much, hand-in-hand.

Greek mariners still trying to return to hearth and home—still trying after three thousand years to return to their wives—to islands that have been lost in time; islands that have been plucked back under the waves...

Inertia leading inexplicably
To a new arrangement. So
Fold me up like a chair, lean
Me against the house, put my
Hair back in order: because
We are all learning to love,
We are all trying, anyway.

NOTEBOOK OF PW [7.13]

I watch you weave in and out of the
Olive trees, your feet bare and light,
The muscles of your voice, singing.

I am like an infant in a swimming pool: a strong
swimmer who nevertheless depends on someone
older to lift him out of the water so that he does not
tire and drown.

The actuality of a difficult concept: growth.

'Do you think Daisy would like me?' she asks
innocently.

All systems fall apart like seedpods.

The brain reads itself, turning its pages over
unconsciously, wanting to reach the next stage of
the story, and so on, until the end.

Lift up the moonlit stones,
Find a white flower growing there:
Take it, call it idolatry.

NOTEBOOK OF PW [marginal commentary]

I am an insightful psychologist, and because of this,
women think they are falling in love with me.

NOTEBOOK OF PW [7.14]

A certain palpable hue—a blueness—that changes
everything.

The night air is full of humor and mortality.

The easy victory of escape has been had.

Experience is defensive.
We are not who we used to be.
Not nearly as brutal.

And her heart was beating like crazy when I put my
hand across it—

Only beauty is implicit in your grace;
Your body formed like an urn
Around the dream I had of you.

And it was strange the way we made love—like she anticipated everything: my coldness, her coldness—our feeling of guilt; our mutual desire to be hurt.

Speech generated by the
Implication of plasticity.
What the soul does for itself
Is survive. The figural unity of a mental
Conception is everything.
[Question. Diminution. Moonlight.]

Love—that massive singularity—that gaping wound in space—

And then there is time, like water—flowing through her hair...

For the Greeks, the tetrahedron was the symbol of the atom, the indivisible unit, because it is the simplest of the Platonic solids: four sides (and below four you can go down to two dimensions).

'The Dancer was not a great book, it was merely sexy,' she likes to say.

Her hands twined through my hair; my heart like a piano broken on the rocks; the music of me ringing everywhere.

Bright water, her hands lifted,
Overturning the cups of heavy flowers,
My darling. Ribbons of grass;
The air and the sea.
Gentle, gentle.

There is something about me that people do not
trust. What that is, I have never been able to discover,
making it impossible to articulate inwardly.

And we talk about this honestly. We have been
more honest in general. Making us more dishonest,
I guess.

Writers who are atheists cannot write about hell,
because they cannot believe in it—what they believe
in is the life of human consciousness, which is
bounded and finite: purgatory itself.

I want to cradle her head in my hands. We are
enclosed in the luminous envelope of a dream:

A daisy chain
To count the days by.
(As if we were counting).

And the old themes (love death the sea the
stars)—all hauntingly sung back to me as if from a
disembodied source.

I am bereaved of you; the nocturnes you
Sang and the dead-black river of you,
Drowned like stars in milk.

We are the unimportant figures drowning in the
background of a picture.

An essay on clarity.
A sterile freshness.
Waking up past noon.
No longer in love.
(No longer).

Permutation poems: all cut up.

Your body has been winnowed down to light;
Secretive, gathered out of elegy.
I grope around you: more than blind.

Careless with eyes, fingers, mouths. Careless,
always.

NOTEBOOK OF PW[marginal commentary]
1: The soul is like dark water at dawn: we exhaust
ourselves trying to fall asleep.

2: Nietzsche's insight that there is in men and women a motivation stronger even than love or hatred or fear—

3: We have nothing to say to each other at last.

4: I'm not sure if what's happening is the projection of my fear or the real thing.

5: 'I wanted movement and not a calm course of existence. I wanted excitement and danger and the chance to sacrifice myself for my love. I felt in myself a superabundance of energy which found no outlet in our quiet life.' (Leo Tolstoy, Family Happiness)

6. I wait within myself like an animal inside its den.

nights negotiating with morning not to come

the herbs around the house growing wildly and Peter wants to dry them to make tea with for a year when he gets back (a sign that he is already ready to go)

the anatomical complexity of connective tissue being the reason I could never paint his portrait (also I cannot paint to save my life)

utterly ridiculous I know: the trivia of trying to fall asleep next to an enigma/idiot/poet

Tonight is total dark—no stars, no moon.

Inner deviation:
Deep in the way of mystical love:
A blank (or node) that we realize is Us.
And we are swept up, then
Cudgeled down.

A love underdetermined like a game of chess. A love that was always there.

The truth is that I need to literalize my anxieties in order to clear away space for their more poetic iterations; if there are any left—and I'm starting to think that, no—that pool has been drained from the bottom.

Daisy and I get along because Daisy treats my moods as she would the weather forecast; as something that determines whether or not she can plan a picnic with the kids. Mariel is NOT like this.

Thanks to Mariel we have an old Olivetti up here now that is much more romantic than a laptop would be. But it doesn't matter because I have nothing new to write.

(I am rewriting The Dancer, I realize).

I feel clean, healthy.

You undo a syllable, you turn it over:
There, the primal scene builds
Itself into an edifice of isolation.

Then, behind me, a wild rose
Begins to bloom: it is you.

I have been taking a bath in the sea every morning.

I have refined you down
Into silence: : the first breath,
The last sheaf of spring.

There is an emotion I escape from, and an emotion
I escape into: these emotions are one and the same.

Andromeda, on the rude rocks, half-
Drunk, having been left by the other stars;
The hornlight wound around the west,
The sun burned into the ooze:
As you are, as you have been, shining.

I should clamber out of doors, over the sea-rocks—
cast myself headlong into the churning headwaves.

But you have this lovely face still—and it is lovely,
so lovely Mariel—this face that I always thought

was kinder than you actually were; less courageous but more delicate.

And this gap—yes, as for this gap: how to close it back up—or how to diminish it; otherwise we'll get stuck in the utter waste of the middle—seeking our way out of the captivity of years and years of ad hoc explanations...

Pulled sideways, the daisy petals, the fringe
Of coronal darkness around your navel:

Daisy and I stopped giving parties years ago, but Mariel and I are tempted to invite teenagers and men and their dogs—

Driftwood fires; teenagers singing and playing guitar on the beach; we go down and try to talk to them; a few speak English; we bring a bottle of wine. I kiss a young woman (who is not beautiful) on the cheek; Mariel laughs at me, walks back to the house; I chase her.

It is foolish to insist on fulfilling sexual relations within the framework of marriage—

Proust begins his masterpiece by bragging about going to bed early—

A series of experiments that culminate in the discovery of an emotional ozone layer .... 'You look tired, or bored or both,' she observed tonight.

A prayer is always a multitude
Of offerings:
A depth which bestows itself on a deaf,
Itinerant divine.

Debussy—stood the tones on their heads; let the blood rush to the tops of the chords.

What we have is common
And unwished for.
A blue cinema: a rosebloom halfway off
Its stem.

Like passages of Chekhov: we are gorgeously depressing.

Drown your hair.
Draw up your head in this, the
Light of intimacy.

'I did not fall heavily, nor did I feel any pain, but I felt so weak and unhappy that I buried my face in the ground: I could not bear the strain of seeing around me the things of the earth. I felt convinced that every movement and every thought was forced, and that one had to guard against them. Yet nothing seemed more natural than to lie here on the grass, my arms beside my body, my face hidden.' (Kafka)

Pull the image from its sheath:
Late summer blues.
Determine its tone by the way
It sings for you.
And feign the mercy of joy;
Wound me with understanding.

Cheese and soggy bread. But we don't question each other's culinary skills; they are good enough for what we need.

'Could you photograph me?' she asks, almost innocently, 'like you used to?'

Draw the circumference of absence: name it Zero.

This summer like a withered tree. A dead emotion. A sentence run on too long.

She paints watercolors in a notebook that are very good. She does everything well, like she always has. And, as usual, she is completely unaware of her own gifts. (Acting is a way of performing her charisma instead of living it).

My own talent is so meager compared to hers—but I work harder for it.

'Do you think Kafka meant the things he wrote in his letters?' M asks.

She feels definite: like the locking up of a house for the night.

We have taken the risk of believing everything we say about ourselves. I'm not sure there is an equal reward for this risk.

She has a genius for living that I do not—

where did our loneliness (pure as spring water) come from?

he was reading The Three Sisters because he said it reminded him of me (and what a woeful thing to be reminiscent of what a sad thing really he's unbelievable I thought)

Masha Masha Masha: why are you crying Masha?

and after it got dark we cooked pasta and drank wine and laid on the floor of the shorehouse for hours and hours and hours talking and talking

but what matters is that we made our attempt (that we

threw ourselves into a field of resistance and were thrown
back down and now that we only have the (aesthetic)
problem of growing old and accepting the backwards
fatality of dying can we really look at each other in a
simple uncomplicated way

'to separate yourself from other people' he wrote (and so
the structure of us broke)

and 'Peter Peter Peter you old fool Peter—'

(I am a hummingbird flying through the eye of a storm)

underneath a tree before the heat of the day I saw him
kissing a very young woman with dark black hair and I
wanted to run and hit her across the face and curse her
but I didn't: I just watched them for a few seconds before
going back to the house and now it is dark and I can only
hear the sea and the sound of his breath rising as he sleeps

NOTEBOOK OF PW [7.18]

She grew up drinking plain water
Because it was best. Love, akesis,
Ruin and desolation. Just as before.
So many times, over the past few years.

Friendship is the ethics of choice.

Our love is like a cathedral on an island with the
tide rising around it.

Each
Of us builds our ground inside
A finite space.
Each of us
Assumes the stance of someone
Who has to build that ground
From the inside out.

What is this darkness whistling through my ears?

The world that passes over is the world
That we stare through. So we gather vowels to
Form a name; gather the rain to acquaint ourselves
With thirst. And You, White Rose:
Will You unlace Your hands to form a church?

I'm spun out of a geometrical proposition: I am the
limit of my own imagination.

*there was no imagining this: the strength of the body sunk
like the moon from sleep suddenly awake*

*the old tambourine of the mouth jangling open/shut to
meet his:*

*'because she loves too much' people've always said about
me ('because she loves too much') without knowing why*

*the passion was so deep in me that I wanted to cry out
shatter the waves stop them in place roll them back to the
horizon*

*I in You: You in I: the sea wiping us clean the salt my
breath heavy with water Your hand in my hair on my
breasts all crying the hope yes of dying (my love)*

NOTEBOOK OF PW [7.19]

Like trying to play the piano but having clumsy
fingers; falling drunk all up and down the scales...

Particles of light shattered, shattering; breathing
the humid storm air. 'It is so lovely lovely lovely,'
she whispers to me.

'There must be something occult in the ground
of everyone; I firmly believe in something hidden
away, a closed and secret signifier, that inhabits the
ordinary.' (Mallarme)

Each tide of breath is an alternative to silence.
Each roseflower is the residuum of transference.

And this is Our universe of obsessive repetitions;
our universe of touch not understanding—physical
sympathy co-existing alongside psychological
resentment.

We come awake at the sound of bees:
The summer eats away our kindness.
And we must learn to talk to each other
The way we want to be heard.

And what matters in literature in the end is surely
the idiosyncratic, the individual, the flavor or the
color of a particular human suffering.

My father did not like my books; he pretended
to, but I knew he was lying. He liked realistically
written novels about realistically drawn people. He
thought what I did, whether in poetry, or prose,
was a trick. And maybe he was right. (I've always
worried that he was right). I do not know why I'm
writing this down now.

Notebooks are always reflexive: they always think
their way back to their own beginnings.

The avenues of cypresses have been burned to
The ground, and one by one, the violets
Must be sheared from the side of the mountain.

Like some astronomer's wife's eyes turned to the
stars she told me she thought poets could shred
clouds; stop time; make their way across the sea by
moonlight—she said that the stars are like ghosts
who do not care about the living.

Time is a relativizing device, because it changes our perspective whenever we apply it to our thinking. We dissolve memory in time, like honey in a warm cup of tea.

Genius perhaps being an undiscovered type of memory (a theory).

(Another theory: of love as squalor).

Understanding a sentence means
Getting hold of its content.
The content, left like a housekey
In the mold, is in the sentence itself.

Vocal chords to create harmony; hands to create; a sea full of pearls—and so to dive or not to dive?— the eternal question of the man who lives alongside a cliff...

NOTEBOOK OF PW [7.20]

A radical testing of an old concept—that our words and the world are one—

A poem is a three-dimensional metaphor.

Your eyes rolled back, your hands
On your breasts, ungraceful in the
Emptying of your desire.

A poem is a sifting agent. A body is a sifting agent. They are both looking for the same thing.

'I'm still afraid of dying.'

I pick blue phlox to crown your wings,
Which like a parasol will open to me.

A cluster of falling stars breaks apart and disintegrates in mid-flight. Life momentarily regains a sense of potential. And her hands in the dark?—I hold them while we're kissing.

Literature is self-defense. It is the evolution of consciousness past the point of despair.

I hear voices of supplications; I feel myself wanting to cry; I want to float like bright deciduous tufts of seaweed out to sea; sink pass the difference between light and dark—piecemeal or not, I'd like to go, float—disappear...

Whose voice is this,
Crumpled in a paper
Emulsion; lost?
Because no one else struggles
For such relief, or has
Retained so much strength
In their hands.

Like a blossom of sea-myrtle throwing sparks from its stamen, like a wave rolling out of a forgotten sea—

I will take you between my teeth
Like the petals of white lunar flowers
And swallow the liquid pulp of you.

There are only projections interacting with projections—desires conflicting merging breaking away from other desires; the night air sweeping through the bedroom, through the kitchen, back out the screen door; gestures, tones, voices—and we're moving across a bleak, uncharted territory. And does she really want to be like one of my affairs? To be like some twenty-three year old graduate student who I have to take out for coffee—does she want me to stroke her hair? tell her how sad it is that things have to end? Because I don't think she's strong enough for that. I don't think she considers these things. And I resent her for wishing everything serious away.

Language is a small, organized revolt against the polis of banality.

Your gypsy mouth, your palms upturned—

Howling is not always identical with singing, but sometimes it is.

And I have this memory of her saying, 'Peter I want to be like a tree that never dies; Peter I want to be roots in the earth'—I have this memory of hearing her say this and wanting to cry—of turning her mouth to mine; of her teeth biting my lip and almost drawing blood; of watching her thin unbrutal body lay trembling in the semidarkness—

And the whole time on this little island, we've been back in New York; back inside our young bodies; back inside the moment right before she met Richard. (And it's from her I learned the art of betrayal).

Richard could handle her better—

Abstractions fall like
Eyelashes from your sweater;
One ankle tangled still in a dress.
And how old are you, that your
English is good enough that I
Can understand you?
(A spark of music passes down your
Throat, like light).

A window rises, a moment comes to pass like a cloud through a mirror. It is so much more beautiful than we thought:

Criticism means hearing music when the music stops.

There is a semantic difference between touch and gesture from a distance. I am learning this more and more.

Curvetting bits of midnight, nettles and rose-sprouts at the edge of the village, hibiscus and grass:

The art of living is the art of feeling everything.

Lamb for dinner tonight, with salt and lemon.

The law is the impulse—

The impulse is the law—

Casting her stars across the
Rimless dark.
Watching them roll off into nowhere.
And who knows when her
Mother will awake and force
Her into ordinary language.

Now: the smell of the open water; thinking maybe this old boat needs repairs; a baseball cap pulled over my brow; feeling harmless and bored and sunburned.

All categories, dichotomies, schools, of contemporary writing are—at best—just heuristic ways of gesturing towards, or away from, the inarticulable matrix of silence that lends human self-consciousness its mass.

Her face, her limbs, tremulous, aching, the smell of apples and lemons, thrusting her fingers through my hair and beard.

'You need instruction in hating falsehood.'

Peter came out of the shower today looking so tan and hale and even though his hair is gray he still seemed youthful and he's just shaved and he's lost a little weight (not that he was heavy) since we've been here (and we've barely been here!) and I have this terrible feeling that I won't be able to be happy by the end of the summer

NOTEBOOK OF PW [marginal notes]
Children pluck fish from the sea.

Mariel undressing in the bathroom, stepping into the shower. Mariel running her hands through her hair—her smiling at me. Her singing. Her laughter.

rejoice/despair: either/or: give/take: open/close: Mariel/Peter

Every moment being a reinforcement of guilt—

My own obsessions coming to the fore—time, language, spirit. The spirit's desire to latch onto SOMETHING; to turn the key; open the door—

A fear of writing literature that has become standard. My consciousness resists me: forces me back into the shape of one who cannot create.

And feeling suddenly ordinary I feel suddenly weak.

(Self-enclosure means 'modern' in literature).

demonstrations of love: pointless heroisms: the hindered initiative of choice:

a blade of seagrass bent between my fingers (I hold on to it I wait for You to come ashore) and Your poems were unearthly to me (and You evaded your life by hiding inside them) and Your absence has thread through me like a needle but I've been sewn (doublestitch) to the air and you said you left your wife but I don't believe you and all my feminine strength is washed unwashed and washed away again and our perfect nearness is ended: the nearness of our isolation each night presents itself to us small and timid like a fish egg and with our awful livid beaks we tear open its pearl-like shell caring nothing for the delicacy

(and he is already up and awake: shaving showering eating defecating drinking coffee reading the newspaper and I'd like to hate him but I don't)

NOTEBOOK OF PW [7.25]

I've been taking a series of black and white photographs—almost like the watercolors she painted in my notebook of the lighthouse—of old men fishing off the piers—and me with my straw hat and worn out tennis shoes looking into the camera (looking into her)—and other things— things that I want to remember; things that I don't want to remember—and then—and then there's the memory of her with a cigarette in her mouth, peeling an orange, afternoon sunlight spilling across the bed, my father listening to a Bach oratorio downstairs, her eyes as black as midnight—the orange between her fingers working itself from its casing—her taking the cigarette between her fingers; greyish smoke blown from her lips; the first orange slice between her teeth—the rind on the bed in the sun, the first slice suddenly cut in half with her teeth—the juice trickling down her chin—

I can only make ironic apologies to M after we are
done fighting, I realize. I am not capable of making
real apologies. I do not want to make real apologies.
She does not deserve them (and neither do I).

Dwelling apart and limitless silences.
Japanese cherries and the commotion
Of angels. Let all this stand out
As symbol. Let's insist next time on
Sleeping.

NOTEBOOK OF PW [7.26]

Paralysis, inhibition.

But seablue again.
Your primitive
Nakedness becomes you.

Less obsessive, less over-compensation.

Terminological problem to be solved: 1) how to
avoid a lie 2) how to lie while avoiding a lie

I do not have the philosophical equipment to
excavate here. The island is dense with concepts
of individual beauty that I will never have time to
understand.

'The endlessness of the nights here is the one thing that I didn't anticipate before we arrived,' I told her just now.

NOTEBOOK OF PW [marginal note]
Devoured.

I want to remake my body to resemble a shield in the sun.

But it is only out of compassion that we went so far away from everyone else to be with each other.

A year from now I will be able to write a book again.

the sea of the past moonlight shining across it and like water from under the sand rushing up to greet us so lovely under our feet and it would be lovely to go somewhere and be alone and it's always easier to love someone who lives outside of the margins of your life (he knows that) someone who doesn't age with you or get angry or frustrated someone who doesn't decay into ugliness and obscenity and ashes and I have this longing to place my hand on the belly of myself as a younger woman where the sap of life ran once: I could take a nail drive it through myself

out to sail this evening and coming back and eating at a

restaurant by the water after the sun had gone down and
the stars come out and the earth itself is a garden he said
the stars falling are just like seeds and I wanted to say to
him 'carry me over the water plant me under the waves'

but just to swim or fish or climb up to the village square
to buy chocolate

earth pigments and volcano plaster brush it with light
place it on the mountains to grow:

honey-pale the webbing of the stars torn out again and
again like orchids picked from the air:

because We must uncover our sorrow like a gift

NOTEBOOK OF PW [7.24]

"Close in a bower of hyacinth" (Keats)
"and a few stars were lingering in the heavens"
(Keats)

M admitted today that she spent an hour on the
phone with Richard—but what do I really care? I
don't at all. It feels impossible that we could have
suffered so much, and loved so much, only to
become so sterile now.

'if extremity of weather had not forced me from the coast' (Walter Ralegh)

But it should be possible to make a clean break of things—shouldn't it?

'And when this is all over, I'd like to die an exemplary death,' she said.

Sea Hymen:
Closed pearl:
We're all
Praying towards high heaven.
(You wrote to me).
Said you thought it was better to
Live unkissed.
And we stacked the waves like
Granite blocks.
(Closed pearl: where are you going?)

And touch is a tearing asunder. An excavation of anger.

And tonight, sitting on the porch, my pants rolled up to my ankles. A single lamp on the table. Deep night; all black—the sea.

She is smart enough to never have to be honest.

The thread from birth to death snaps like a suspension bridge in a storm.

And a lifetime exploring a single emotion yields: ?

In between any two rational numbers, a cluster of irrationals grow like weeds.

My hovering life: like a speck of moonlight in a glass of water.

The assuredness of a great heart: that is what I want.

The Phoenicians' hands are unwrinkled;
And their hunger terrifies you
Because you know that they remember you.

Big sparks of rain today.

All I want, I realize, even now, is to write.

After dinner she told me stories from the theater—as usual. My favorite part of the day—always my favorite part of the day. The least obsessional. The healthiest.

A gypsy girl parallels
The eroticism of

Your wife coming
In through the door.
A sense of color, so
Catch the sunlight in the hair.
The summer was very great,
And lord, it's time.

the rhetorical structure of everything you say is like a honeycomb: geometric and multi-dimensional: and we are both trying to inhibit our general tendency to speak in metaphysical terms when we talk about our love

NOTEBOOK OF PW [7.26]

Again, having to listen to her on the phone with her son for hours—I blame myself.

I only mention it because the sound is so strange, so unlike the sound of the sea; an incantation, coming through a voice and a body.

Have been reading Homer every morning and night; the winedark etcetera—

Physically exhausted.

Her face was pale as paper tonight. We didn't kiss before fucking this time. 'Because grace allegorizes itself as pain.'

Cut the white laurel into pieces.
Bath me in seasalt.
Cleanse my skin of forgiveness.
Acrid summer. Final loneliness.
Unclose, Flower, strange angel.
Remembered and forgotten
At the same time.

NOTEBOOK OF PW [marginal note]

I don't understand where it comes from: the-depth-from-which I-speak.

everything down to this question of self-esteem (that I do not have it) and to this question of why I am so desperately desperately desperately in love with him and the answer then: because I can steal his blind self-assurance for myself

simply moving through sentences like a fish through the shallows

answering questions that only he can ask: why are we encoded in each other like genes?

NOTEBOOK OF PW [7.26]

She complicates things: she wills the complications.

You spread yourself like jelly over
The rocks. You remove your idea from
The cast of the body: the transition is
From knowing to unknown. Unknown
To the bitterness of late arrival.

There is no consolation in a contradiction, I'm
aware.

We make love. We talk about the future—but what
will this lead to?

Returning to our spouses having had our fling...
and I want to protest against this, but?

'I'm willed away like a headcold and you've just got
to decide to accept my ironies or to reject them and
accept that we'll never see each other again and that
our lives will be permanently unconverging.'

Tend to this light like a flower.
Because we are still here
Among the disbelievers,
Our singing voices bruised.
And the oranges are on the table,
And they are still vulnerable,
(And they will be devoured).

'In your experience, is it possible to platonically share a bed with someone you're attracted to?' she asked me while we were making dinner.

Later, I told her about an Italian graduate student I was in love with for several years when I was in my late thirties. 'It's funny,' she commented, 'how you remember certain things so clearly and forget others so well.'

I have no confidence in anything I write anymore.

NOTEBOOK OF PW [marginal note]

The priest of the body is the tongue not the heart; not the unwombed brain of dirt and flowers.

'I never wrote for anyone except you' he said and I almost believe it

because I don't sense that he is over the possibility of fucking other people

and neither for that matter am I

NOTEBOOK OF PW [7.27]

My only longing is to retrace a few steps. To see those seablue eyes of hers open again to me.

The fisherman arrive on the shore
And put down their baskets. Under
The trees we will eat until dark.

Swam in the sea this morning—leapt from the rocks
under our house. (I write this now while it is past
midnight and the morning seems impossible).

My violence is introverted: within, it merges with
the way I speak (to her).

'You blame me for all our tension,' she said today.

I know that I am, pragmatically speaking, unfree.

In a moment of lightness
You are engulfed and I spit you,
Seedless and mystical, into the earth.

The language we speak together is mined from old
modes of living. Words from long ago; selfsong,
mere motion; the sea turning on the axis of a
sinewave.

Ibsen is truly astounding. There are four playwrights
for me, obviously: the Norwegian, the Russian, the
Englishman, and the Irishman. (This is what we
talked about today).

I want to be like a fish gutted on the deck of a boat:
bone sinew blood all.

Took a photograph of a tiny blue flower growing
between two rocks—and God knows what I see in
nature; what nature means to me; and being so close
to Mariel day in and day out I wonder whether we
will have to turn to God again and to nature to find
some kind of freedom of expression—

We harness this momentum as it swings through us.

A loaf of black-bread, coffee, milk—

There you are again,
Perched on the rocks. Elegies
Unstopped:
Pouring from your lips like rain.
And sung like this? My god.

Language is a miracle inside the blue of the sea
outside.

*when I look at him as he walks toward me (or watch his
eyes and his nose and his lips contract when he cums)
then there is nothing else (and it's a singular happiness
connected to him because of him and it is the fullest
happiness and it is so full of potential) and now Peter
getting better at his cooking (fish in lemon sauce with
garlic)*

calling for a leap into the future: when we are a bit older and the infinity of sorrow narrows as it approaches the open ocean:

NOTEBOOK OF PW [7.30]

Mariel talking about the death of her sister from cancer. How little she felt. How it was like a great sigh of relief (Clara's death). And why do I feel accountable for everything bad that has happened to her?—maybe because she expects to incorporate her pain into my pain. (Probably).

We have masks for every hidden, hostile intention; of which there are many.

I want an etymology of glances.

Both of us are trying to undo thirty something years of pointless hurt, I realize...

And I don't blame her for her obsession with her mother. It would be healthier to forget completely; but obviously: forgetting anything about childhood is impossible.

A girl with tiny hands, tiny knees... a road with cypresses.

A blind man stands on a bridge, looks at the entrance to the underworld: he sees the blue plumes of a flower on fire.

Remove the husk of optimism from the stars, and let them just float up there, lyrical and nameless and free.

Images become so dense
(Inside) that they cannot
Be penetrated by thinking.
The ears ring, sound
Continues far away.
And everything is beautiful
On the page. Every word.
Every evasion.

Hillsides of snapdragon and lily of the nile and dark-purple lavender. Picking, drying certain flowers for tea like we learned from the locals.

Have ridden my bike into town every day this week to chat with a girl, Maria, who waits tables at a village bar and speaks good English.

(And self-knowledge is always a confession, I think).

I hurl myself into the endmost of time through its vast tracks of unsealed paths of stars: and we reflect the

universe's carnage (he and I) through our bewildering
seachanges: having loved and given up and loved again

so from within I project I open our fingers aching our
mouths aching everything aching: and how romantic we
are even now at our age

and it feels like we are like chains of islands connected
underneath the ocean floor and I hear myself whispering
yes with him whispering transcriptions of my inner life
of (calligraphy sewn into air) and the nights here make
death seem like something we created to fill in the time
before time: when people were ancient and unconscious
and free and I think that he and I (that people) should be
entirely particular to themselves: mirrors for every kind
of loveliness: mirrors for silence: mirrors for faith

NOTEBOOK OF PW [8.4]

Not that I'm capable of it anymore—a clear
emotion—and not that I'd want it—

Because love alone is life—

'I have always regarded the neurotic as a failed
artist.' (Otto Rank)

Not without changing, not without faltering, not
without repenting—

Elements erased.
Worlds remade
From string and light.
So drag me under
The waves: pull me down to
The central place of This,
The word's conceiving.

I have never trusted people enough to be honest with them; I have always reserved my honesty— held it back threateningly.

'I'd love to have some sort of exchange with you, but I can only do so, happily, if you don't insist on being as patronizing as you were just now and have been in the past.'

NOTEBOOK OF PW [8.5]

We sealed our hope in each other: now we are vessels of that hope.

A moment of rupture: the dead past recognizes no continuity with the present.

the basic movement of self-denial is self-reflection: prior even to doubting and question: just looking in

but I've always been the short-circuiting type: I've always been prone to cutting off the electricity by accident

*and are we sincere? from moment to moment? that's all
I've wanted to ask*

NOTEBOOK OF PW [8.6]

Dinner of fish with garlic and butter and a salad on
the side.

What Kafka wrote: 'From a certain point on, there
is no more turning back.'

If the tense organizes time—what does time
organize?

And we talked about retracing, about magical
transformations of the past.

'I am devoted to your anxiety,' she said.

'The more indirect I am, the more you seem to care,'
I said.

(We maintain a certain reserve towards the real
world).

'The conversation was heading in a direction I
wasn't particularly eager to pursue.'

All rises and moves like the
Bones of the body itself when the
Skin clings to it as a shadow.
And now the music is over.
The string-quartet has gone to bed.
Slip out your dress, Lightfoot'd.
Waste your life,
Wait to be born.

NOTEBOOK OF PW [8.7]

A flower known as ranunculus.

Densely ruffled blooms; tubers like fingers.

Receive water
From a nectar bowl:
Water in a phase of white.
Link it back gently to
Our beautiful emptiness.
Unseen. Vast.
(All this is necessary).
Our gift. Your spring.
A handful of
Greek flowers.

Spent the day observing a few boats. Sketched the
clouds, the water, the dunes. Lay out in the sun
until I was almost burnt black. Thought nothing;

felt nothing; wanted nothing; was nothing myself.
Said nothing to each other—made love after making
dinner.

A kindness receives you only
To let you go;
Cherishs you like an only
Daughter. And your
Obedience is a kind of resignation.
But we won't again, we
Promise, we won't.

NOTEBOOK OF PW [marginal note]

'Psychologically the notion of genius, of which we
see the last reflection in our modern artist-type, is
the apotheosis of man as a creative personality: the
religious ideology being thus transferred to man
himself.' (Otto Rank)

NOTEBOOK OF PW [8.8]

The double of a vacuum inside
This single self:
Damned fool, twilight;
Lavender leaves and the glisten
Of August rains.
Unspoken ballet, yes.
And miles of wind.

I want to talk until we are too exhausted to speak.

I've chosen the wrong technique for the novel I have not even really begun: narrating only the most spectacular of events and mangling temporality in the process.

This is the creation of new values from immense suffering—

This is a question of love,
Of seeming too ordinary to see
What happens when
It happens.

In Proust knowing people is often very much about dealing with the anxiety that one can't control them.

Talking about visiting the coast where Shelley washed up, under the mountains of Carrara, where the marble comes from.

A strange language
You steal from the birds,
You strike their
Throats like flint;
You steal their fire from them.

How do I know the next sentence I write isn't going
to lead me off the edge of a cliff?

We are all fables of unwritten being:
Never too goodnatured to slip the
Straight jacket of the sun and reinvent
Our nakedness.

A ship in the midst of the sea.

(?)

'There's no middle ground anyway and you've
got to make the terms stark if you really want to
understand what they are.'

NOTEBOOK OF PW [8.9]

Our crisis is that the sea grows dark,
That the houses along the beach
Are inhuman and inhospitable.
So put the lamp back on the table.
Break the world into pieces.

Spoke to my daughter on the phone today. My son
won't talk to me, neither will Daisy, obviously. And
I regret this only enough to write it down.

I am standing at a distance from everyone: which is
to say that I am alone, but still upright.

Cut wax flowers for a vase; she says she adores them.

Just as you used to be, skin like
Roseleaf, hands given over to the
Music of poetry.
Now we sing like fallen angels
On the rocks,
And cease to be ourselves.

And yes I went to see Maria too; and in a sense I
have been going to see her my whole life.

'A novel is meant to make you feel things for its
characters as if they were actual humans, you can't
be so clinical.'

NOTEBOOK OF PW [8.10]

There isn't a blank space in which the judgment
happens, there's a ready-made space, a judgment
already there that you either live up to or don't.

Time is something that one
Must strain from language like whey.
A denser pattern
Of singing eventually evolves into poetry,
But a poem
Stretched out too far becomes a
Salience unlike
Any other kind of prayer.

There's something about Greek that seems to go deeper into words than we're used to.

So come Lazarus,
Speak to me from your redemption,
Live the wild life of a saint.
Burn these offerings. Place yourself upon
This altar of mercury and flowers.

NOTEBOOK OF PW [8.11]

Beach heliotrope grows just fine in a coastal garden beset by salt spray, bearing bright purple flowers all summer.

The surface of erotic language is rough
Like pearl. Unveiling
Yourself in the sonority of
Breath. Unglutting yourself
Of broken vowels.

There's a foreground here, no matter which way you look.

NOTEBOOK OF PW [8.12]

Like an interpretation of quantum theory, we are here and not here at the same time.

'I wonder if simply knowing that's what we both
would have wanted was enough to make it feel as if
it had happened.'

And obviously,
God is a process of assumption:
He is a clean, starless night.
(Because His heart has shed
Its golden petals).

'Do you really feel it's some sort of love you feel for
most women you become involved with?'

'I dont like that I'm a theoretical figure for you;
you've been testing me out in your head for years.
I'm like a romantic science project.'

NOTEBOOK OF PW [marginal note]

Understanding at the root
Of your beautiful fury,
Lifeless, laying in bed
Like that, with your
Hands over your eyes,
Begging to be left like
A puzzle there—
So incomplete.

NOTEBOOK OF PW [8.14]

And by staying here, you are blessed.
Where the moon rises.
Where the stars fall in ornamental
Showers.

NOTEBOOK OF PW [8.15]

Unceremonious: but greet me anyway.
Lay across our bed like an old dress.
Because O' unruly child, you've
Stripped me of my voice.

But don't be so unkind that I can't
Stand you, please.
Otherwise, you may do what you want
With me.

Watch: your mother fold her hands over
Her dress. And go to sleep then, while
Everyone is still dancing.

NOTEBOOK OF PW [marginal note]

Floating nocturnes out the window like balloons.

Blue of the seablack nightflower.

I've always been bitterly jealous of writers who have
had more success than me.

And when the poem ripples from your hands
Like a butterfly, you say
That you are a poet,
Or are you afraid to believe
That sex is like religious life?

Curl the moon into a Japanese lamp: weave it like a
golden thread into the dark.

Consistency of voice is a lie. But the lie evolves too
fast for us to notice it. (And life is so much easier if
lies are believed).

Understanding gravitation analogically by achoring
the concept to instances of attraction in one's own
experience: assuming for the sake of argument that
gravity and love are the same phenomenon.

Last summer, when you kept
Your hair unbound, and when
I was unrecognizable. Nothing
Protects us from the lamentations
We hear crying from underground;
Because a god speaks through us
And our love involves the love
That came before.

NOTEBOOK OF PW [8.17]

Went for a walk with Maria far from view of the cottage.

(I do not feel shame).

NOTEBOOK OF PW [8.20]

This sweetness is like a hand that brushes away a crumb.

NOTEBOOK OF PW [8.24]

Our bedside manner (our careless devotion to one another) is the only ethic that the universe expects us to uphold.

NOTEBOOK OF PW [8.30]

I have been so fucking afraid—so fucking afraid of loving people and of missing them, and I can't forgive myself anymore for that fear.

you (noontide) rush over me and You (Peter my love) curse me with your violence

and I come back into the room and think: Peter is thinking about a younger woman Peter is thinking that he made a mistake Peter is thinking that he misses his wife his kids his life and the way he looks at me (coldly/

warmly/distantly) from the table where he writes under
the kerosene lamp makes me think that yes this is true
that his betrayal of me (or his unbetrayal of himself) is
evolving in front of me like a storm (clouds gathering
growing heavy scattering rain across the ocean) and I'll
never never never tell him how insecure he makes me feel
(and he can guess he guesses he knows) and I'll never say
what I'm thinking about because I'm too afraid of what
he's thinking (how we never should have run away like
this (like we were kids)) and that whatever future we
have is closer to a kind of pleasant congenial friendship
and how unforgivable that would be to me (if he asked
me to be his friend) because that's nothing no one could
ever want because what we want is to control and be
controlled

NOTEBOOK OF PW [9.2]

We've exhausted every kind of mercy—and good
riddance.

My novel washes away like a sandcastle at eventide.
But I never had any intention of doing serious work
here—or maybe I did—I never know—I just don't.

'There's this French book by Marcel Pagnol, I
remember I told you about him when we first met
actually, in which these older characters essentially
talk about the way they fucked up in terms of love,

seduction, etcetera when they were young because of their pride.... And they're so old and there's nothing beautiful or sensual about them anymore, so it's sad and sweet and a little bit funny.'

I like the feeling of salt drying in my hair; the wind on my face when I ride my bike into town, or along the boardwalk.

The astronomer cannot follow the
Frequency of images into the dark.
Now, let us fold back the trope
Like a dog's ear on the page.

Maybe we are headed towards the affectionate sympathy of old age; but then again, I doubt it.

What I like about Maria is that she seems genuinely interested in learning new things.... She is not passive either: she displays an awareness of nature that is startling and active. (She intensifies; she concentrates).

Papering over mysteries. Measuring the skeptical distance that separates me from her: and the possibility of her (and even as I write 'her' I do not know to whom I am referring... perhaps both of them).

Halfmoon made with a paintbrush; Eros the Greeks
called it, the bittersweet—and we broke each other's
hearts—

And the humbling silence
Of bird, beast, and flower:
This is what you called poetry.
The archaic rippling
Under the surface of art.

Draw a circle I tell myself: stand in the center as if
under protection.

A notebook is like a glass fragment.

Life's happiness is a particular place.

Integrity projecting itself
Over the mass of compromise
And finding that there is no
Scandal in destruction.

NOTEBOOK OF PW [loose sheet, fragment]

Split open the throat of a seabird: stole the silver
bulb of its music.

I refuse the tragic:

The capacity to create: the capacity to see the
beautiful in things; the stars, the sea.

Overcoming of emptiness within emptiness.

Night blackened-sea.

Because everyone wants to be lied to.

A letter from Daisy. (Nothing is irreversible).

into the water the water which you only hesitatingly went into earlier because others did: the water that you were afraid to go into but now NOW because you run from something you hate MORE you overcome your fear you willingly DIVE into the water: you choose it you choose change: and complete submersion and letting go: you choose the terrible/beautiful flow of destruction and being born again and again

NOTEBOOK OF PW [9.3]

The nudeness of you that I pressed
Like a rosepetal into a bar of soap.

The rocky beach is empty.

Our plumage fallen off,
Our skin rough and moonmarked.

The flight of the old gods, the sound of the sea, the beautiful sorrow of coming here with her; touching her, remembering her, understanding her—fatal and irrevocable.

Thinking: I have nothing new, nothing that must be said, written, expressed in anyway. I can only pantomime my youth (my lust); my creativity in general.

And of course, she's obsessed with Daisy, and everything that constitute(s)(d) my marriage to Daisy. And what can I really tell her? Daisy's favorite brand of coffee? the particular and utterly consistent smell of Daisy's shit after she's done using the bathroom every morning?

'You always seem sad, genuinely distraught over the fact that some people think you mean badly when you are just being honest Peter.'

When left alone to my thoughts I am a good person and an inquisitive person, a person capable of reason. When with other people, I am not—I am only capable of pretending.

The world as I see it today: full of wondrous clarity, of concrete desires, discrete understanding.

Or maybe, again, the issue is just that I feel ontologically spent: empty in that pool that once spilled over into language.

Prizes make life simple when you know exactly what you're going for.

NOTEBOOK OF PW [9.6]

Walked up to the village bar and sat drinking with the other old men. I've learned enough of the dialect now to say simple things. And it is easier to be yourself when you have less words at your disposal, I've learned.

NOTEBOOK OF PW [9.10]

We were blindfolded, before we were
Allowed to step back into the world.
And yet, you kept pointing towards the
Water as if you could see it. No one
Cares for the almond flowers anymore,
Hovering like lights over the sea.
And the blue of your hands
Inside mine is like coming awake:
Cherish me, I want to say: tell
Me this bitterness is over.

NOTEBOOK OF PW [marginal note]

There is still a last step to take—to be taken—to subsist on the level where Love exists and Time does not pass.

And listen! the sound of the sea heard with eyes closed
listen! listen! the wind and the sea like static bits of a
piano in the night and I will drift out out to sea out out
out to sea: moving towards silence towards that charcoal
black that music at the end of the movie and in the
morning we'll watch the long-legged birds dissolve into
rain over the water and this is the way a true divinity
appears the villagers say (soft silent on the feet of mercy)
and tonight is moonless starless completely dark and only
the barest outline of objects are visible (the sea and the
dunes) and I can hear you breathing faintly holding me
in your arms and 'open like a shell and let me devour you'
you say and I want to know if I've given something real
to you other than selfishness and self-deception and the
seawind (do you remember? the seawind drove us over
dunes and swept through my hair and I was sixteen and
we walked at daybreak along the water not having slept
our hands were interlaced like roses withering and falling
and clustering again in the waves) and I want this to
be like a last quartet a last movement before the dying
fall and I want to find the symmetry between notes (the
emotion that music discloses) and nothing is ever enough
not for us and you say that time is like a fissure of light
through rock and you were there (and I was there!) when
time deposited us like silt on the floor of eternity and our
hands curled (floating above us): and look! all the stars of
the west are falling my love and 'no I wrote those poems
so that one day you would find me' and your eyes are

made of oriental paper waiting to be folded and it doesn't matter if you've aged or if I've aged because each of us is a thread a melody a chord and a trillion years will pass and the sun will explode and we'll be back again at the same note having saved our best melodies for last (and rosy-fingered my love I was born out of the night and you were like no one else: and my dead wings were taken up in the wind because I was your devotion and you sunk your teeth into my muscle and drew out the sweetness and you opened me and you prized me apart and tossed me back into the sea and Peter: when we made love it was as lovely as a sonata between piano and violin).